Captain Abney

Instantaneous photography

Captain Abney

Instantaneous photography

ISBN/EAN: 9783742840417

Manufactured in Europe, USA, Canada, Australia, Japa

Cover: Foto ©Andreas Hilbeck / pixelio.de

Manufactured and distributed by brebook publishing software (www.brebook.com)

Captain Abney

Instantaneous photography

INSTANTANEOUS PHOTOGRAPHY.

BY

CAPTAIN ABNEY, C.B., R.E., D.C.L., F.R.S.

NEW YORK:

THE SCOVILL & ADAMS COMPANY OF
NEW YORK,

60-62, EAST ELEVENTH STREET.

1895.

LONDON
CARTER AND CO., 5, FURNIVAL STREET, HOLBORN, E.C.

PREFACE.

—◆—

THE writer published a series of articles on instantaneous photography in PHOTOGRAPHIC WORK some short time ago, and these have been re-cast and added to in the present volume, to form the second of the series of Photographic Primers. He trusts that in the pages which follow, the fruits and the results of much experimental work will prove of more than transient value to the readers. His desire has been to show that whether the unit of time of exposure be a second or a hundredth of a second, the same rules have to be followed to secure the best results, and that it is worth considerable labour to ascertain what exposures are really given when an instantaneous shutter is employed.

South Kensington, Aug. 1st, 1895.

INSTANTANEOUS PHOTOGRAPHY.

CHAPTER I.

LET us just for a moment weigh the claims put forward for ordinary photography to be considered a fine art, and we shall then be in a position to see in what respect instantaneous photography differs from it—not in any carping spirit, but in the light of the common sense with which we οἱ πολλοί are endowed.

When the reader speaks into a graphophone or phonograph, the vibrations which his voice makes are imprinted on a tablet, and from this tablet what has been uttered can be reproduced mechanically; but the soft modulations of the voice are absent, and there is wanting a "something." So, in a photograph, it seems to the writer that there is the same absence of modulation; the beauty which the sentient being bestows is wanting, the picture is mechanically impressed on a non-sentient surface, which will give a print with a deal of the poetry of an artist's drawing left out. What the piano-organ is to the piano, so it appears is the

B

photograph to the artist's sketch—there is the want
of expression in the former which is present in the
latter.

This is a bad beginning for the subject in hand, but
it really is not inappropriate, for taking this view of the
subject, the practical making of instantaneous photographs cannot be the low form of photography which
some believe it to be. For our own part we believe its
results give greater pleasure to more people than do the
more carefully planned photographs. It must not be
considered for a moment that an instantaneous photograph gives of necessity the idea of motion. As a
matter of fact, it is often grotesque, and conveys the
idea that figures are posed in attitudes in which they are
never seen, and it is their very grotesqueness that often
makes them the most interesting, and it might often
be added, comical. The attitude of a man who is
caught whilst walking, just touching the ground with
the heel of the preceding leg, for instance, is never
associated in the mind with progression; nor do the
sharply defined spokes of its wheels give the idea of the
rapid bowling along of a hansom cab; and yet both of
these are seen in instantaneous photographs. They
open out to view what would be seen if the eye were
totally differently constituted, and could distinguish
attitudes taken up for, say, a 1-100th of a second. As a
matter of fact, the eye can scarcely distinguish between
two attitudes which are separated by the 1-10th of a
second, if so much, and those attitudes which make
the most impression are those which change least
rapidly; and where these are depicted, the idea is given
that motion is taking place. Making allowances for the

fact that instantaneous photographs do not see moving objects as the eye sees them, they may yet give scientific information, or may amuse, though they may fail to instruct in art.

It may be well to explain at the outset that the epithet "instantaneous," as applied to photography, is, of course, incorrect. A photograph taken by a flash of lightning is not instantaneous, for the exposure takes a time which is not beyond the limits of measurement. The word, however, has come to be recognised as applying to photographs taken with very short exposures; in fact, any exposure varying between about the 1-5th of a second and the 1-2,000,000th, which last is about the exposure which is required to take a photograph of a bullet in its flight, may come under the head of an instantaneous photograph. It is to such brief exposures that we shall address ourselves, and endeavour to show how the best use is to be made of the appliances which photographers have available for the purpose.

The first essential for instantaneous photography is a lens that will work with a fairly large aperture; if it will work with a stop inserted, which is 1-6th or 1-8th of the focal length, so much the better; but it is available if it will only work—that is, give a fairly defined photograph—with 1-11th of the focal length. Some people imagine that a lens which will work without any stop whatever is the best to employ. But this is a mistake if it be a doublet lens, for if the track of the rays be considered, it will be found that the plate will inevitably be better exposed in the centre than at the margins. The reader must remember that there is often a fixed permanent diaphragm in the centre of the lens. When such a diaphragm exists, it is not a lens which can be used with full aperture.

The diagram will show why this is. Let L be the lens, and P the plate, and let us consider a point in the margin C. The only part of the front lens which will admit light to C is the small portion *a b;* the rest, *a g,* is

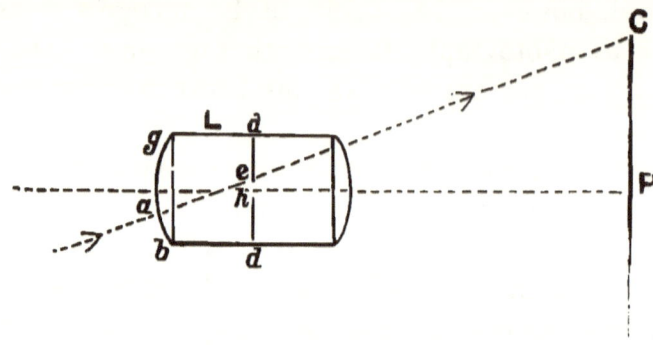

Fig. 1.

absolutely useless. At the centre of the plate the whole of the lens *g h* will be utilized, and consequently the centre will be much more exposed than the margin of the plate. If, however, we insert a diaphragm *d d,* having an aperture *e h,* which just allows *a c* to pass, it will be seen that the central illumination is reduced closely to the same as the marginal. Hence, in such a case, to secure equal illumination, a diaphragm is absolutely necessary. When choosing a lens for the purpose in view, we must bear this in mind, and it will be found that a lens whose components are close together—that is, with a small separation between them —will be the best lens to employ ; for the diameter of the diaphragm that may be used will be larger the less separation they have. This must, however, always be coupled with the proviso that the field is a flat field.

A flat field to a lens means that the curvatures and the refractive indices of the glasses used have been properly chosen, and it is only necessary to look over the long lists of lenses which are made by different opticians to convince oneself that there must be lenses which have various states of perfection as regards this flatness of field. The photographer, however, should be able to choose for himself, and this is very readily done if he obtains possession of the lens for trial. When the writer obtains a lens for this purpose, he always tries it at $f/8$ and $f/16$. Now, a lens which can take a picture which includes a wide angle, say 65°, may be taken as a rule as certain not to cover the full size of plate with the first-named aperture. The margins will be seen to be wanting in definition if the central part is in good focus, and *vice versa*. Hence, for an instantaneous picture, it is better to include a more moderate angle than that, say 50°, when it is probable that very many lenses, which would be unsuitable for a plate of the full size they were intended to cover, will give a sharp, or, at all events, a very fairly sharp picture with a smaller sized plate. Thus, there are several lenses extant which are intended for a 5 by 4 plate, which, with an $f/8$ aperture, will not give marginal definition, and yet will satisfactorily cover a quarter-plate; and further, in which this aperture would cut off part of the lens from work with the larger plate, whilst with the smaller it would be effective throughout. Suppose a lens of this kind had to be tried, we should proceed as follows. Put the lens on a whole-plate, or 7½ by 5 camera, and mark in the centre of a glass plate a rectangle of 5 by 4, and of 4¼ by 3¼. Focus an image of a distant landscape (with not too much near foreground) on the ground glass, and then place the marked glass in the slide, with the back and the front opened. The lens will now be exposed to view. Place in it a stop $f/8$*, and see if from the 5-inch boundary any portion of the lenses of the doublet is cut off by the mount. It is evident that for this size of plate such a lens cannot be satisfactorily used with that diaphragm. Next, place in the slot of the lens the next smallest diaphragm, and again note whether any of the front or back lens is cut off. If it should be, put in the next smallest, and continue these observations until the stop is found in which the eye sees only glass through the diaphragm when it is placed against the 5-inch mark on the glass plate. Note what diaphragm just gives this result, and remember that for a satisfactorily evenly-exposed picture no larger stop can be used with that size of plate. Repeat the same observations from the line which marks the 4¼ inch by 3¼ inch boundary. It will, of course, be found that a larger stop may be used in this case than when the lens is viewed from the 5 by 4 inch line. If, as before said, the lenses are not widely separated and of fair diameter, a stop $f/8$ should answer the test. There are lenses which are very small in diameter, sometimes the diameters of the components themselves being smaller than $f/8$. Of course, such a lens, though, perhaps, useful for ordinary work, should be immediately rejected for the purpose before us.

Supposing a lens fulfils this first condition for a quarter-plate, the next thing to do is to take a negative of the accurately-focussed landscape, with the $f/8$ stop inserted,

---

* Thus, if the focus be 6 inches from the diaphragm to the ground glass, the diameter of the stop should be 6-8th inch (or ¾ inch).

in order to ascertain if the photographic focus is equally as good, better, or worse than the visual focus. It is well to take a large sized plate for this purpose, as by holding masks cut to the different sizes of plates against the negative it can readily be ascertained over which size the field is sharp. With a lens to cover a 5 by 4 plate, a quarter-plate should be almost perfectly sharp if it is to be of any use for instantaneous work. Next insert a stop $f/16$, and see how much better the focus is than with $f/8$. Everything ought to be absolutely sharp to the naked eye, and if examined by a focussing glass it should still remain sharp, and bear enlargement, if desired. When $f/16$ is employed, all reasonably near foreground should also be in focus—in fact, everything beyond 20 feet. With $f/8$ this cannot be expected; we must be content if the sharpness is good for everything beyond 40 feet. There are some cheap lenses which never give sharp images photographically, alter the focus as you may. They can be used with a very small stop; but for instantaneous work they are perfectly useless, unless by those who dislike anything at all sharp in a picture. As far as the other qualities of a lens are concerned, we need not pay much attention to them. If symmetrical, we may be tolerably certain that they will give straight and not curved lines, as the images of straight lines at the margin of the plate. The colour of all the glasses used by opticians is very uniform throughout, and it may be taken for granted that no very great difference will be found in it, and that therefore one lens will not be much more rapid than another from this cause. The thickness of the glass used has also very little appreciable effect, unless it happens that it be yellowish, for it will be found experimentally that a very thin layer of glass will diminish the light causing the photographic action almost to the same amount that a thicker layer will do—of course within rational limits.

It may be as well to mention that the negative which has been supposed to be taken will also show if the lens gives what is called a flare spot—that is, a circle of increased deposit at the centre of the field. The flare spot, it may be observed, is due to a reflection of the aperture of the stop, of which it is an enlarged image. Opticians, however, now thoroughly understand the method of making this flare spot cover more than the whole of the plate. Although very appreciable when concentrated as a small patch, when the light forming it is extended over a large area it becomes so attenuated in intensity that it is practically absent. A flare spot is always exaggerated in effect when the lens is dirty; and talking about dirty lenses, it must be remembered that a dirty finger-marked lens will cut off and scatter as much as 50 per cent. of any light which endeavours to pass through it. This is a point regarding which photographers often pay but very little attention; but want of cleanliness often has a serious effect when making very rapid exposures. A very wholesome piece of advice to give to photographers is, to clean the lens frequently, and not to take it for granted that it is free from dirt.

CHAPTER II.

As we have commenced by treating of the optical part of the apparatus necessary for instantaneous photography, we shall next consider the method of giving a rapid exposure by means of what are called instantaneous shutters. Perhaps on no pieces of practical apparatus have more labour and thought been expended than on these. They are often constructed on very beautiful and ingenious designs; but, in many, something is wanting, and they are often far from what we may call ideal shutters, whilst others are as nearly perfection as may be.

The first question is as to the best position that the shutter should occupy. It is evident it may be on the front of the lens, at the back of the lens, or occupy a position close to the diaphragm ; or, again, it may be placed close to the plate. Let us see what these several positions entail in regard to the general exposure of the plate. We will suppose for the moment that the shutter is of a guillotine type, and that it falls from the top to the bottom, the exposure of the lens beginning first at the top, and finishing at the bottom. When it is in front of the lens, as the top part of the lens is that with which the image at the top of the picture is made, it is evident that the sky of a landscape is first exposed, then the middle distance, and finally the foreground near this base. Or let us take an example of the figure of a man moving across the view, and whose image occupies nearly the total height of the plate. The hat will be first exposed, then the face, next the trunk, and finally the legs, the last portion which is impressed being the feet. The photograph would not represent him in the position he occupied at any particular instant of time, but it would represent the position that his hat occupied at one instant, his face at another, and so on. Suppose the guillotine was a fairly narrow slit, which moved downwards at a moderate rate, it is evident that the movement of any small portion of the image would be small during exposure, though the motions gone through between the time the hat and the feet were exposed might be large. In fact, it might happen that the image on the plate would show the man as tumbling backwards, and the relative position of the swinging arms to that of the legs actually reversed, and make the proportions of the figure absolutely untrue.

With the shutter at the back of the lens the attitude of the man would be reversed. It might show him as in the act of falling forward, for the image of his feet would be first exposed, and the hat last. Of course, these are exaggerated examples of the want of truth that might be exhibited, but they are possible.

With the shutter close to the plate the distortion is much more likely to be marked than in either of the above cases, for even with a guillotine shutter on the lens in which the slit is moderately narrow, the image seen through it at one instant includes more than that

width, for, were this not so, the image would not be of
bigger dimensions than the lens itself. With the shutter
close to the plate, on the other hand, it is the width of
the slit which determines the amount of image exposed.

A   B   C

Fig. 2.

The accompanying silhouettes show what happens when
a narrow slit passes across the plate. A is the image of
a man actually photographed with a shutter at the
diaphragm. At the proper distance from the lens this
image was made to move at the rate a man would move,
and exposure given to a plate with a guillotine shutter
next the plate, the slit being narrow. B is the photograph obtained of A when the figure was moved in the
direction he faced ; and C when the motion was in the
reverse direction. B looks tumbling forward, while C
looks tumbling backward.

When the shutter is placed near the diaphragm the
conditions are totally changed. The exposures for all
parts of the image commence and finish together, and
are of precisely the same duration. If it be necessary to
give a certain exposure to an image, for satisfactory
results, it is manifest that it does not matter theoretically

whether the whole image is exposed for such time, or whether the different parts are exposed successively for the same time; but it matters a good deal practically, for the total time occupied in giving the successive exposures must necessarily be longer than that in which the exposures are given at the same time; and if the camera be held in the hand, the probability is that during the longer total of successive exposures a greater movement in the hands of the operator will be found than during the shorter and simultaneous exposure.

The accompanying cut shows the movement of a hand-camera in a quarter of a second. The top line is the movement when held in both hands without any support; the second line shows the movement when held under the chin and above the chest. The third line shows

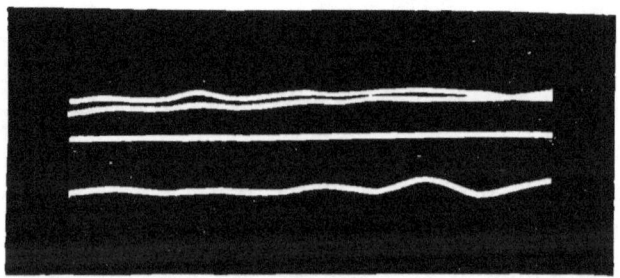

Fig. 3.

practically no movement. In this case the camera was held in two hands, and supported on an umbrella handle. The lowest line shows the movement when held against the bottom of the chest, so that the beating of the heart and the breathing interfered with the steadiness. The writer cannot help thinking that the diagram is very instructive, and shows that practically perfect steadiness can be attained by the use of a support.

These records were obtained by fixing a vertical card, in which a pinhole was pierced, to the camera, and allowing the light from a stationary lamp to send a beam through the hole, the image of which was focussed on a plate moving horizontally.

On the ground, then, that distortion, and also total time of exposure, is minimised when the shutter is placed at the diaphragm, the writer has come to the conclusion that practically that is the best position for it. Another point is this : that the movement necessary in the shutter itself is less in this than when in any other position, as the diameter of the diaphragm must ordinarily be smaller than that of the surface of the lens or plate itself.

Let us now consider as to the circumstances which favour the movement of a camera when held by the hand, owing to the release of the shutter. In the first place, it must be borne in mind that the camera and shutter are practically one structure, and that when the shutter is placed ready for exposure, the combination has its centre of gravity in some one position. If, when the shutter is moving, the centre of gravity shifts to another position, a movement, slight though it may be, must take place unless the camera be rigidly supported. There are two ways of meeting this difficulty : one is to make the motion of the shutter symmetrical on each side of the lens (in other words, to close to the centre) ; and the other is to make the movable parts of the shutter as light as possible compared with the camera. Now most shutters are light, but there are many which do not close centrally, and, in fact, as we shall see shortly, such a method of closing is detrimental, except when it is placed at the diaphragm. Another point is, that the release of the shutter should be as light as possible, and should not be by a push or pull, but by a *pressure*. All rifle shots know that the sights of a rifle are invariably moved from the mark if the trigger is pulled, whereas when a pressure is applied between the thumb and finger this does not obtain. The release, then, should be by a pressure, and all other methods should be avoided. With the pneumatic arrangement, of course, this does not apply, for the release is then given by an apparatus which is not rigidly attached to the camera. For hand-cameras, however, the pneumatic release is inconvenient, though it can be effected by inflating the tube by the mouth instead of by pressure with the hand.

As regards the efficiency of a shutter, the question is as to how it is to be judged. It is not difficult to understand, if we have two shutters, both of which give the same total duration of exposure, that if one leaves the full aperture of the lens uncovered for double the time that the other does, the first one will allow a greater quantity of light to reach the plate, and will, therefore, be more efficient than the second. In other words, the efficiency of a shutter depends on the ratio of the time during which the plate, or part of the plate, receives the light coming through the full aperture, to that of opening and closing. Perfect efficiency, of course, would be when the time of opening and closing is *nil*, and the full aperture is used throughout. If this theoretic efficiency could be secured, it is manifest that it would be immaterial whether the shutter were at the back, the front, or in the centre of the lens. In comparing the efficiency of one shutter with another, the standard that is taken as unity is the theoretical shutter, but every part of the plate has to be considered, unless the shutter be placed at the diaphragm. What we have to determine, then, is the aperture uncovered during every small interval of time, to add these apertures together, and divide by the total duration of exposure, and compare it directly with the full aperture. Thus, suppose the total duration of the exposure was the $\frac{1}{20}$ second, that

At the $\frac{1}{200}$ of a sec., $\frac{1}{10}$ of the area of the aperture was [uncovered

,,	$\frac{2}{200}$	,,	$\frac{1}{5}$	,,	,,	,,
,,	$\frac{3}{200}$	,,	$\frac{1}{2}$	,,	,,	,,
,,	$\frac{4}{200}$ to the $\frac{6}{200}$, the whole aperture was uncovered.
,,	$\frac{7}{200}$ of a sec., $\frac{1}{2}$ of the aperture was uncovered.
,,	$\frac{8}{200}$	,,	$\frac{1}{5}$	,,	,,	,,
,,	$\frac{9}{200}$	,,	$\frac{1}{10}$	,,	,,	,,

The efficiency would be $(\frac{1}{10}+\frac{1}{5}+\frac{1}{2})$ 2+3, or $6\frac{2}{5}$ approximately, whilst the theoretical perfect efficiency would be 10. The relative efficiency would be $\frac{6\frac{2}{5}}{10}$, or ·64. If the areas uncovered for another shutter of the same speed were respectively $\frac{1}{20}$, $\frac{1}{10}$, $\frac{1}{5}$, $\frac{1}{2}$, 1, $\frac{1}{2}$, $\frac{1}{5}$, $\frac{1}{10}$, $\frac{1}{20}$, the efficiency would be only ·27.

If a plate, therefore, with the first shutter was just enough exposed, with the second it would be greatly under-exposed.

CHAPTER III.

It is much more simple to ascertain the total speed of a shutter than it is the efficiency, but presuming that this first is known, a good idea may be formed of the latter if the construction is carefully considered. No elaborate apparatus is required to find the speed of a shutter, and any amateur may carry out the measurement in a simple manner : first, without any appliance whatever; and second, with an apparatus which can be readily constructed. Let some kind friend stand at, say, some 20 feet away from the operator, holding in his hand a roll of white paper, and swing his arm round in a circle in good daylight, so that one revolution is completed in one second, and then let an exposure with the shutter be made on this subject. The developed image will show a movement of the white roll, and if the shoulder be taken as the centre of the circle, the breadth of the image of the roll can be measured at the circumference. Another photograph of the same object when the arm is still will give the true breadth of the image. This breadth also can be measured, and the last measurement should be deducted from the first, and this will give the amount of movement which some one point has made during the exposure. The circumference of the circle will be found by measuring the distance of the shoulder from the extreme end of the roll of paper, and multiplying this by $\frac{22}{7}$. Having got the circumference, the movement of the point at the extremity of the white roll is divided into it, and this will give the fraction of a second during which the exposure lasts. Let us take as an example : the width of the image of the roll, which when still is $\frac{1}{10}$ of an inch, and when moving $\frac{2}{10}$ of an inch. The motion of any point at the extremity is, therefore, $\frac{2}{10}$ of an inch. The length of the radius of the circle from the man's shoulder to the end of the roll is $1\frac{3}{10}$ inches; the circumference is, therefore, $\frac{13}{10}$ by $\frac{22}{7}$, or close upon $8\frac{2}{10}$ inches. There are 41 times $\frac{2}{10}$ in $8\frac{2}{10}$. The speed of the shutter is, therefore, $\frac{1}{41}$ of a second. By this plan the rapidity of a shutter can be very readily measured to within a small fraction of the truth, and will suffice to give an idea of what objects can be photographed by it without movement being too palpably visible. But we shall return to this directly.

The next method is more elaborate, perhaps, but it is very exact, and is fitted for a studio where experiments can be well carried on. It is on the same principle. A small white sector is pasted on a black disc of about 8 inches diameter, which is attached to a spindle, as described in the figure, and is attached to a clock-work arrangement, or can be rotated by hand.

The period of rotation may be once per second exactly; but so long as the period is known it does not signify what the speed may be. This period can be very accurately ascertained by noting how many revolutions are completed in a minute. In a case in point it was found that $72\frac{1}{2}$ revolutions were made in 60 seconds. The time of each revolution was therefore $\frac{60}{72\frac{1}{2}}$, or $\frac{83}{100}$ of a second. The method of procedure is exactly as before; but if the camera has an adjustable focus, it is well to place it some 6 feet off, and make an exposure during a revolution. The image made is of the kind shown in the accompanying figure. The angle through which the

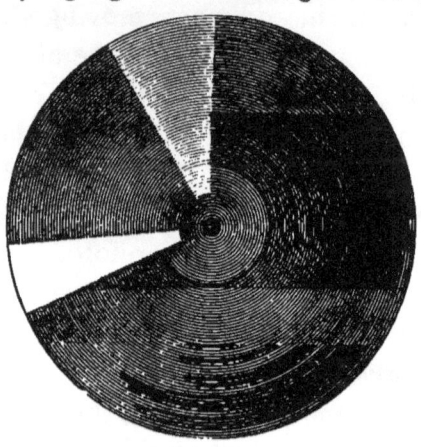

Fig. 4.

arm moves is measured by an ordinary protractor; or, better still, a white circle, with every 1° marked round, is placed behind it, or in front of it, and the amount of movement is read off; the width of the tongue of white which revolves being also noted and subtracted from it. In the figure two exposures are shown, one in which the white sector is still, and the other when it is in motion. It should have been stated that, in the first method, the protractor can also be used efficaciously; but in this case the angle subtended by the edges of the roll is subtracted from the angle of the edges when in motion, and this angle divided by 360° gives the speed of the shutter.

In the case quoted this angle was found to be $9°$, and $\frac{9}{360}$ is $\frac{1}{40}$, which is the fraction of the second during which the exposure lasts, which is closely that arrived at by the other plan suggested.

Before going further into the method of measuring rapidities and efficiency, it may be useful to ask what rapidity is necessary for various moving objects. First, it is necessary to remember that if any point in an object is represented by a disc about $\frac{1}{100}$ of an inch in diameter, it is sharp to the eye. If, therefore, all movement of the object can in the image be confined to this amount, it will appear sharp. Now, with a hand-camera, the focus of the lens is usually about $5\frac{1}{2}$ inches—let us say 6 inches. At 50 feet off, therefore, an object may move through 1 inch and still appear sharp — that is, the motion during the time of exposure may be that amount. Say that the time of exposure is $\frac{1}{50}$ second, it is evident that the object at 50 feet off may move at the rate of 50 inches —say 4 feet—a second to fulfil the conditons. Now, a man may walk two steps of $2\frac{1}{2}$ feet each in a second, and supposing he moves uniformly across the view, he would just move a *little* too quickly. Let him be 100 ft. away, and he would be well within the limit laid down. If he were approaching or receding from the camera, of course the circumstances are changed, and the movement he makes in regard to the plate would be a slight up-and-down motion, and no movement would be perceived until he was quite close to the operator.

Let us take another example—an express train going about 40 miles an hour. During one second it moves about 60 feet. If it be desired to take this at a distance of 100 feet away whilst rushing across the field of view, it is not hard to see that a movement of 60 feet would require a rapidity of exposure of $\frac{1}{750}$ of a second. If it be taken at a distance of 750 feet it would fulfil the required condition with an exposure of $\frac{1}{80}$ of a second. Express trains have been taken, but as a rule they are coming in a marked degree towards the operator, which immensely reduces the apparent motion. The motion of a breaking wave is small comparatively, and it will be found that for pictures of this description $\frac{1}{10}$ second is not too small an exposure with a lens such as is used with a hand-camera. It must not be inferred that this is recommended, but only that such can be given without any great loss of sharpness. For street views the shortness of exposure should only be limited by the rapidity of the plate and the ratio of the aperture of the stop to focal length that can be secured. There are scarcely any shutters which expose more rapidly than the $\frac{1}{80}$ of a second, though, of course, there are some; but none that the writer has used is less than the $\frac{1}{1000}$ of a second, and this is a very rapid rate. This remark only applies to shutters placed at the lens itself, and not to those next the plate. These last can be made to expose any part of a plate for almost any small fraction of a second by narrowing the slit which passes across it.

When instantaneous views are taken with lenses of longer focus, of course the limit of motion in an object is narrowed down proportionately; that is to say, with a lens of 12 inches focus the distances given in the examples must be increased proportionally, or doubled. This shows that in the quarter-plate picture it is more easy to secure sharpness than in, say, a whole-plate picture, since the focal length of the latter is, as a rule, longer than that of the former.

We may as well give a rule to find what motion is allowable. Divide the distance away of the moving object, in feet, by the focal length of the lens in feet, and divide the product by 100, and it will give the result in inches. Thus if an object is 90 feet away from the camera, and the focal length of the lens is 12 inches (or 1 foot), the object may move $\frac{90}{1}$ by $\frac{1}{100}$, or $\frac{9}{10}$ inches during exposure. To ascertain if the shutter is sufficiently rapid to be within the limit, divide the allowable movement in feet by the rate of movement in feet per second. Thus, with the above, if the object were moving 10 feet a second, the speed of shutter required would be $\dfrac{\frac{9}{10} \times \frac{1}{12}}{10} = \frac{9}{1200}$ of a second, or about $\frac{1}{130}$ of a second, a time too small for most shutters. If sharpness be required with a shutter giving an exposure of $\frac{1}{50}$ of a second, the object should be taken at $\frac{130}{50} \times 90$ feet, 234 feet off, or in round numbers 80 yards off.

CHAPTER IV.

We have now to explain how the exact qualities of a shutter may be ascertained. The apparatus which is necessary is not in reality very expensive when the simplest form is used, but is rather more complicated when the more easily-calculated diagrams are produced.

The evolution of the system employed may be of interest. Let us suppose we are dealing with a central closing shutter outside the lens; evidently we can throw the image of the diaphragm of the lens on a sensitive surface, and if that surface be made to move—no matter how for the present—whilst the shutter is making an exposure, we shall get a blurred long image. If, however, we fill the aperture with a card and pierce holes round its circumference, instead of a blurry image we shall get as many lines of light as there are apertures in the card. The length of these lines will show the time during which each of the small holes was open. Evidently each pair of holes which lie in a line parallel to the edges of the moving part of the shutter will have the same length of exposure, and so would a hole in any part of the line joining them, and consequently at the point where the central line of the diaphragm cuts it. It follows, therefore, that as much information will be given if we use only a slit running down the centre of the diaphragm, and instead of a series of lines we shall have a plain figure formed by successive images of such

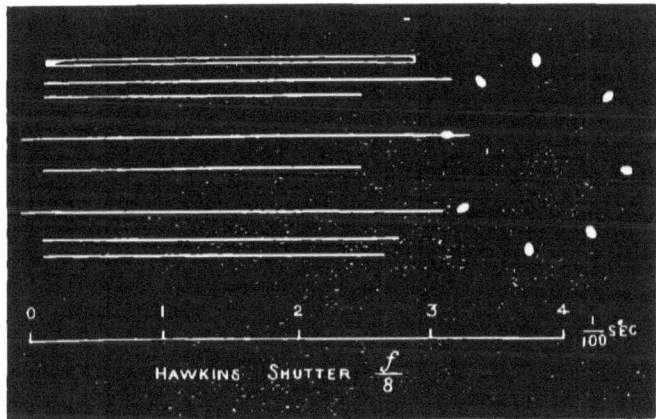

The lines show the diagram drawn by the holes, which were also photographed with the drum at rest.

FIG. 5.

a slit. Or we may take the shutter by itself, and place in the length of its aperture a card in which a narrow

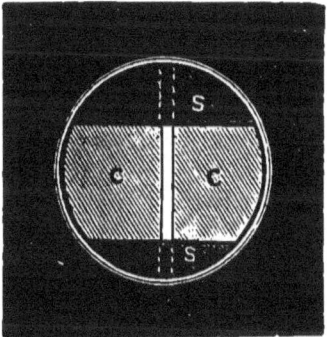

C C is the card in the aperture of the shutter, with a slit cut in it of $\frac{1}{30}$ inch
S S the shutter in the act of closing.

FIG. 6.

slit is cut at right angles to the direction of its motion; we can illuminate that slit by a condensing lens, and focus the beam at the same time on a photographic lens, which will form an image of the slit on a surface placed at the proper distance from it.   When the shutter is released, the slit will first be uncovered, and then gradually covered up again (see fig. 6).   If, as before, the surface on which the image of the slit is cast be moved, we can get a diagram of the slit showing what parts are un-covered at every part of the drop.   If the velocity of motion of the receiving surface be known, we can tell at any instant of time the amount of the slit exposed at that instant.   In some experiments the motion given to the plate was circular.

The apparatus was as follows :—A circular plate, A, on which is placed a carrier for quarter-plate, or a 5-inch

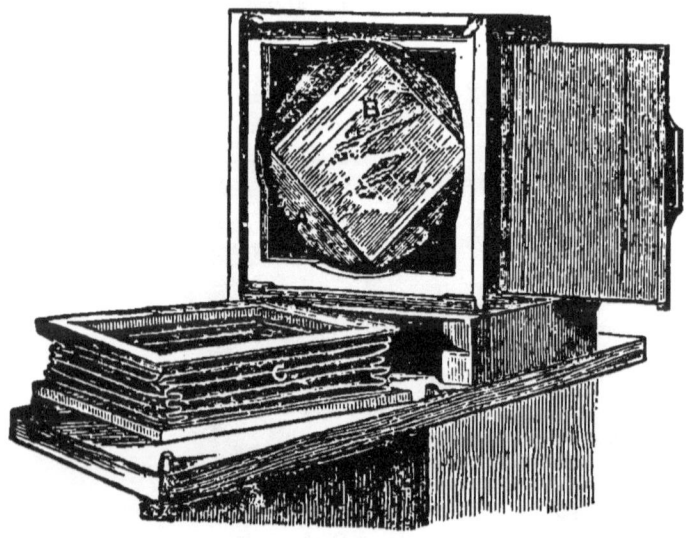

FIG. 7.

square plate, B, rotates in a dark slide by means of a spindle coming through the back of A. To this spindle an ordinaay handle may pe attached, or a pulley which may be attached to it, and the disc be rotated by any mechanical means, such as a multiplying wheel, or by an electromotor. This dark slide can be placed in an ordinary camera with its plate ready for rotation. For convenience, a bellows, C, for attachment, is useful. To ascertain what the shutter will do, a lens is placed in the camera. At a distance from the camera, and in the axis of the lens, is placed the shutter, with a fairly narrow slit placed close behind it at right angles to the movement of the shutter wings, and centrally. This slit is brought to a sharp focus in the plane of the plate, and is arranged so that the prolongation of the image of the slit would fall on the centre of rotation of the plate. Now, suppose that an exposure is given to the image of the slit whilst the plate is rotated : it is evident that we shall have a circular ring, the breadth of the ring being the length of the slit's image. If, however, the shutter is let off whilst exposure is being given, we shall have the ring incomplete. We shall first perceive the bottom of the slit, then its length gradually increasing till the shutter is at its full aperture, and then see the length of the slit diminishing. Such a negative will give all the information necessary as to the efficiency of the shutter, supposing we know the speed at which the plate is revolving. The question is, how to ascertain this. The simplest means that the writer knows is to cause a cardboard wheel, with a convenient number—say six—of spokes in it, to revolve in front of the slit (see fig. 8). When a bright light—which is, by the-bye, necessary to form an image that can be developed—shines through the slit, the spokes of the wheel cut it off at regular intervals, which show in the negative as places of no exposure. These intervals can be counted, and if the

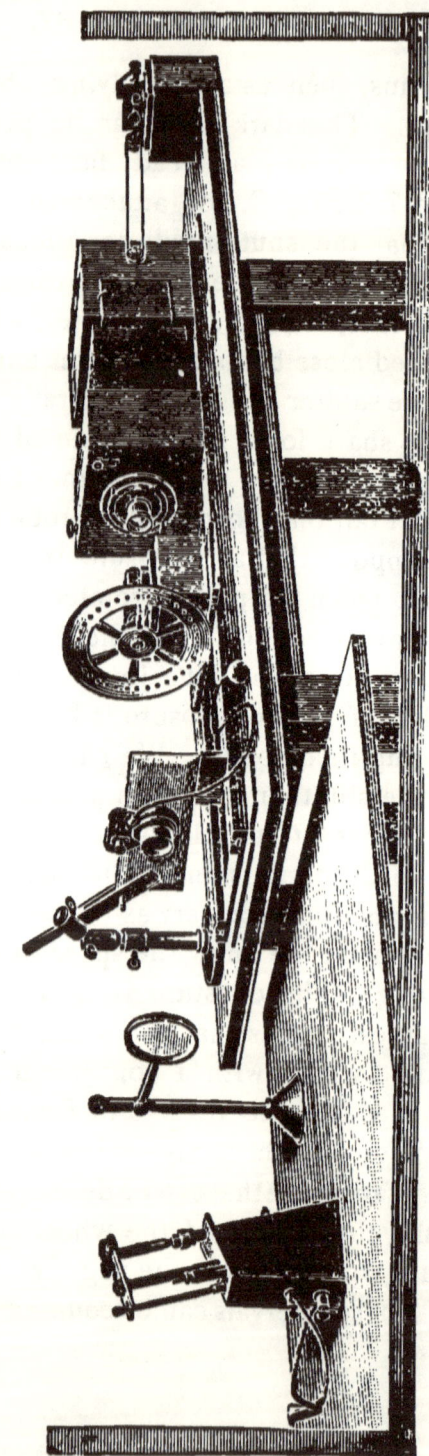

Fig. 8.

number of times the spokes of the wheel pass across the
slit be known, the duration of the exposure is at once
ascertained. To ascertain the velocity of this wheel, all
that is only necessary is that the rim be pierced with
holes, about 3-16ths of an inch in diameter, at equal
intervals apart. This forms a syren, and the musical
note it gives when a current of air is blown through a
small glass tube against the holes tells the velocity of
rotation. The writer has made his wheel to have six
spokes, and 36 holes in the rim. It is about 8 inches in
diameter. It rotates on an electro-motor, and usually
gives a note about E. The pitch can be compared with
the note of a penny whistle, which has, of course, been
previously tuned from standard forks. We give a list
of the number of vibrations per second—that is, the
number of times a hole of the syren passes in front of
the tube through which the air is blown to sound the
note commencing with middle C.

	Scientific scale.	Society of Arts scale
C	512	528
C sharp	540	559
D	576	594
D sharp	600	622
E	640	660
F	683	704
F sharp	720	745
G	768	792
G sharp	800	837
A	853	880
A sharp	900	932
B	960	990
C	1024	1056

There are, of course, other temperaments, the "Diapason normale" having for C 522, the Philharmonic C is 535, and Broadwood's is 546. It will be found that using either of the two given will not make any serious difference in the results, for it must be remembered that each of these numbers has to be divided by 6 to give the number of traces of the spokes per second.

If E be the note, 640 holes pass through the current of air in one second, or that $\frac{640}{6}$, or 107 spokes, pass across the slit per second. Supposing the shutter opens and closes in the $\frac{1}{20}$ second, 6 intervals of non-exposure will be found in the negative obtained by it.

The following is a diagram obtained from a drop-shutter, with the motion accelerated by means of an elastic band.

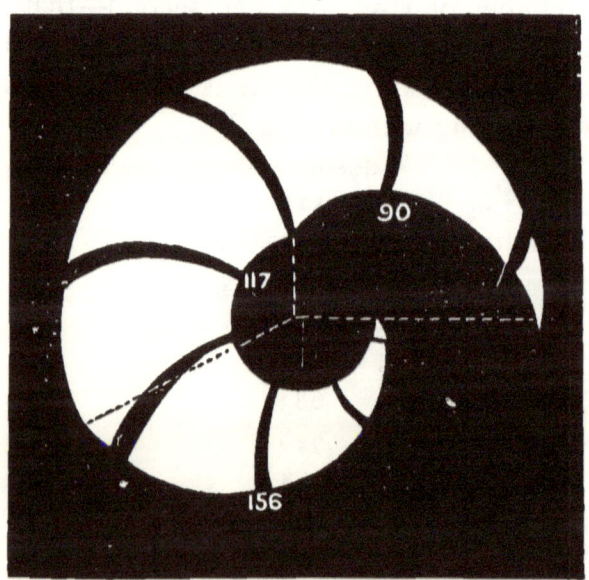

Fig. 9.

It will be noticed that there are $7\frac{1}{2}$ intervals of exposure shown. The wheel rotated 20 times in a second, as ascertained by the syren, and consequently the number of non-exposures per second was 120; the total duration of the exposure was therefore $\frac{120}{7\frac{1}{2}}$ or $\frac{1}{34}$ second. The form of the figure is curious; but if the inner portion of the circle bounding it were spread out, so as to be equal to the outside circle, and the figure straightened, we should have an easily-read shutter diagram. As it is now, we must take the angular measure of the figure—that is, we must see what proportion the full exposure of the slit bears to its opening and closing. We can then form a fairly correct idea of the efficiency of the shutter. In the case before us, the opening took 156°, the full aperture was uncovered through 117°, and the closing, 90°. These angles represent $\frac{1}{79}$, $\frac{1}{108}$, and $\frac{1}{137}$ seconds respectively; that is, the efficiency of the shutter was considerably less than the theoretical one, which would be represented by the total exposure of 363°, multiplied by the length of the image of the slit. The shape of the diagram shows that the top part of the slit was exposed at a different time to the bottom part. If, therefore, the shutter were fixed to the front of the lens, the top and bottom of the plate would receive the full exposure at different times, and the liability to show the distorted motion of an object, to which, in a previous chapter, we have called attention, would be present. Again, it must be remembered that the aperture of the lens with which the shutter would be used is circular, and that the time of opening and closing is therefore the opening and closing of a circular aperture. As the boundaries of the figures, when opened out as described, are nearly straight lines, and as the full aperture is a circle, the efficiency when the full aperture is uncovered is measured by its area into the time during which it was open. The efficiency during the opening and closing will be represented by the length of the exposure occupied in so doing multiplied by half the area, as this last gives the mean aperture. The rule to apply to ascertain the total efficiency of a shutter is to add to the time of full exposure half the times of closing and opening, and to divide the result by the total time of exposure. We have here a ready means of finding out this most important quality of a shutter. In the case in point the efficiency is

$$\frac{\frac{1}{66} + (\frac{1}{79} + \frac{1}{137})\frac{1}{2}}{\frac{1}{34}}$$ or about ·7. If a diaphragm be

inserted in the lens, all we have got to do is to put the shutter, during the experiment, on the lens, and focus the slit, as before, on to the plate, and repeat the operations just described, with the slit, however, across the diaphragm. We shall then get a diagram of the movement of the shutter, and can calculate the efficiency in the same way. It will be found that the smaller the diaphragm, the more efficient is the shutter; and it can be readily seen that, when the diaphragm is a pin's point, the actual very nearly approaches theoretically perfect efficiency.

It may be interesting to show the appearance of the diagram when pinholes are pierced in a card filling the aperture, the piercing being round the diaphragm. In the case in point, six pinholes were pierced at equal intervals round it, and a central one was also added. The conditions of the exposure were precisely the same as when the slit was used, though the plate revolved

.a little slower. The intervals in the broken lines show

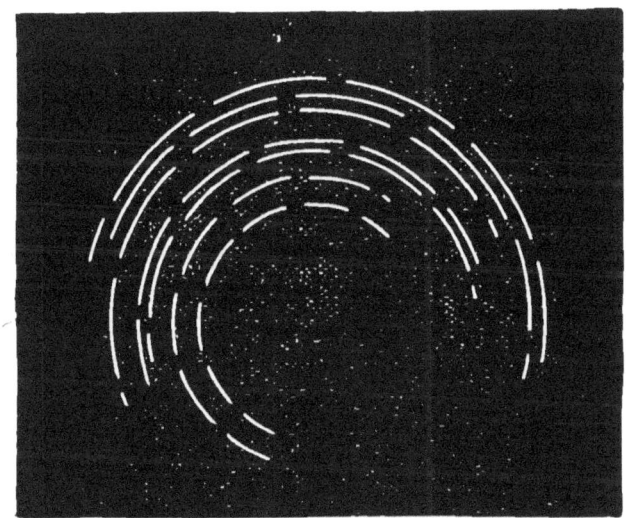

FIG. 10.

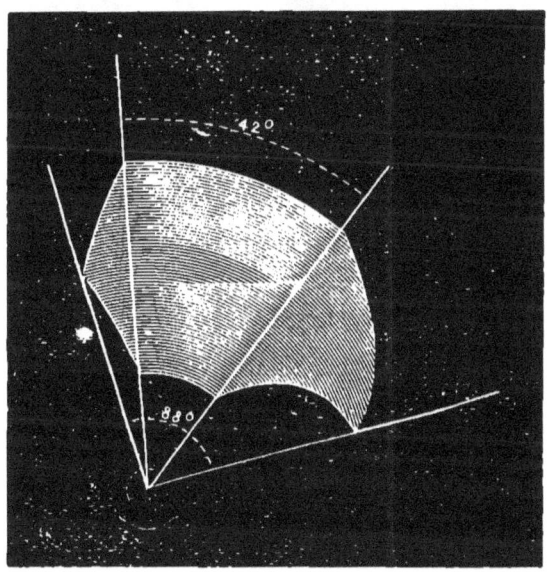

Key shutter diagram.

FIG. 11.

the times when the exposures were stopped by the

rotating wheel placed in the beam.   The middle line is
that given by the exposure through the central pinhole.
The readers may trace out for themselves which is the

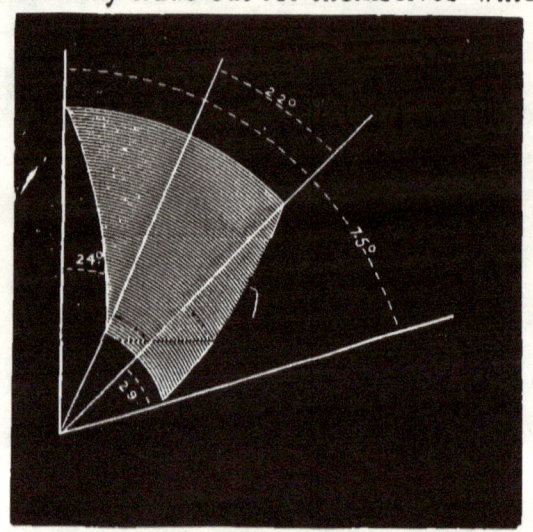

Drop shutter diagram.

FIG, 12.

top and which the bottom pinhole.   It will be seen at
once that the figure is much less easy to deal with than
when one central slit is used.   Figs. 11 and 12 show
diagrams taken in the manner before described.   The
velocity of rotation was, however, arrived at by a method
which will be subsequently explained.

CHAPTER V.

THE most convenient method of getting a shutter diagram, however, is by means of a rotating drum. The figure illustrating the drum is inserted here in order that a comparison may be made between the two methods employed. In this case the procedure is exactly the same as before, only the shutter is placed so that the

FIG. 13.

line of motion is horizontal, and the slit is placed, as before, parallel to that line, so that the image falls horizontally on the middle of the drum.

D

A celloidin film, or a sheet of bromide paper, can be wrapped round it, and secured by a collar fitting tight at one edge, and by an elastic band at the other. The diameter of the drum was exactly $4\frac{1}{16}$ inches, and allowing for the thickness of the film, its circumference when charged with the sensitive surface amounted to almost exactly 13 inches, and this length of circumference was taken as sufficiently accurate when the revolutions were counted or known by the note given out by the syren. If the drum revolved twice a second, evidently the surface moved through 26 inches: if three times, 39 inches, and so on. In a large majority of cases it made 100 revolutions in 27 seconds, or 3·7 revolutions in one second ; that is, it travelled 48 inches in one second, so that in $\frac{1}{100}$ second ·48 inch passed a given spot. Evidently with this speed of rotation any moderately short exposure could be measured. When the exposure was too long for this speed, a fly-wheel of cardboard was attached to the spindle of the drum, and, according to its weight, so was the speed reduced.

The image will be the same as if received on a flat surface moving uniformly up and down, the drum being only an artifice to secure this. It has already been

FIG. 14.

said that if the figure taken on the rotating plate be straightened out, we shall get a diagram which can be easily measured. The accompanying figure is a diagram given in the last chapter so straightened, being taken on the drum. It will be seen that the shutter was set slower, 10¼ intervals being seen instead of 7½, for the " wheel" was rotating at the same speed as before. The efficiency calculated by adding the time of exposure during which the whole aperture was open to half the time during which it was opening and closing, and dividing the same by the total time of exposure, is ·66.

In some cases where the jaws of the shutter are not straight—as, for instance, in a Furnell shutter—it is useful to take diagrams with the slit at right angles to the direction of motion, as well as parallel to it. This enables a graphic method of estimating the efficiency to be adopted, instead of what becomes a rather laborious calculation. Fig. 15 shows the diagram

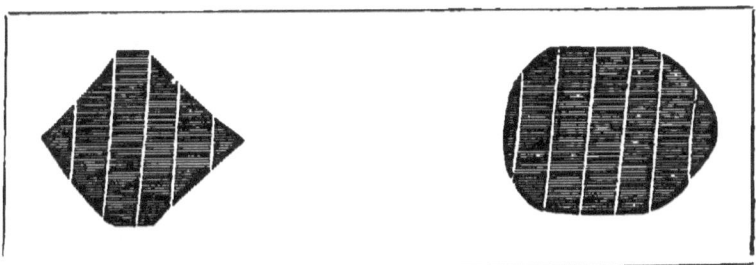

FIG. 15.

of this shutter taken as above. By simple measurement, the aperture of the shutter at any instant can be known, the one figure being a check upon the other. Fig. 16 shows the apertures at empirically fixed intervals. The syren also tells us that the number of revolutions of the drum was 22 per second. The time interval between two ribs being known, and being a certain distance apart, and the circumference of the drum being also known, it is easy to calculate the speed of rotation.

One other very simple plan of getting the number of revolutions of a wheel is to attach it to a counting machine. We have used for this purpose an old turnstile counter. It registers units, tens, hundreds, thousands, and ten thousands. By noting how many numbers are registered in a minute, the speed per second can be readily found.

A time-scale can also be impressed on the plate with the diagram, by means of a tuning fork, to which a

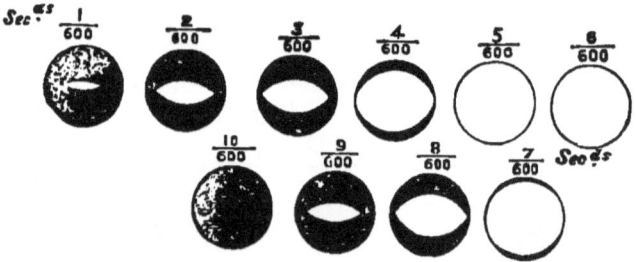

Aperture at different periods of the exposure.

FIG. 16.

light card having a narrow vertical slit cut in it was attached, the slit on the drum being horizontal. By a lens an image of this vertical slit was made to fall exactly in focus on the horizontal slit, and after a diagram had been taken the fork and lens were placed in position, the shutter closed, and another exposure made. The small square bright area made by the intersection of the two slits gave a sinuous line on the moving surface due to the fork's vibrations. The number of vibrations per second being known, that line became a scale.

Fig. 17 will give an idea of the arrangements adopted.

L_3 is a 12-inch R.R. lens screwed into the door of a
dark room, within which the drum and the motor were
placed at a proper distance for the focus. (In the later
arrangement the use of a dark-room for exposure became
unnecessary, the drum being attached to a camera.) Outside E is the electric arc light, and L_1 is a lens throwing
an image of the white-hot positive pole on a circular
aperture in the one end of a collimator (which is simply a
tube with a lens at one end, and the aperture at the other

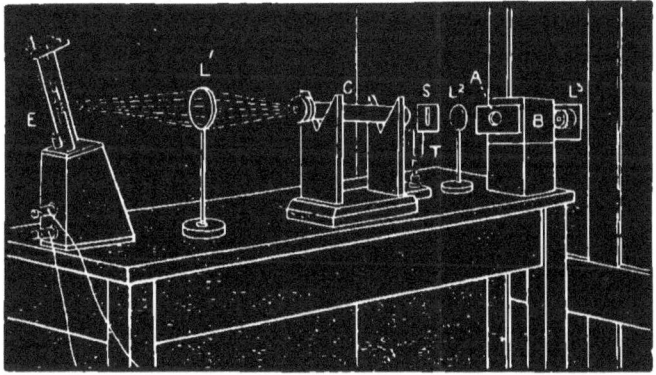

Apparatus for making a parallel beam pass through the shutter and the
camera lens. It also shows the tuning fork in position.

FIG. 17.

placed exactly at its equivalent focus). The rays issue out
of C as parallel rays, and if T and L_2 are out of the way,
fall on the lens of the camera B through the shutter, and
practically form an image of a distant point. The rays
pass on to L_3, where they are collected, and form an image
of the aperture of the diaphragm in the camera lens. In
these experiments the diaphragm was filled with a thin
card, in which a slit was cut traversing its horizontal
diameter. Thus a horizontal line of light was thrown
on the drum. The drum being set in motion, a couple
of exposures with the shutter were made, and it then

became necessary to put the time scale on. T is a tuning fork, attached to which is the card, in which a vertical slit is cut. The card S is placed in the path of the beam as shown, and a sharp image of the vertical slit thrown on the card fitting the diaphragm. Thus a single very small square of light reaches the drum, and

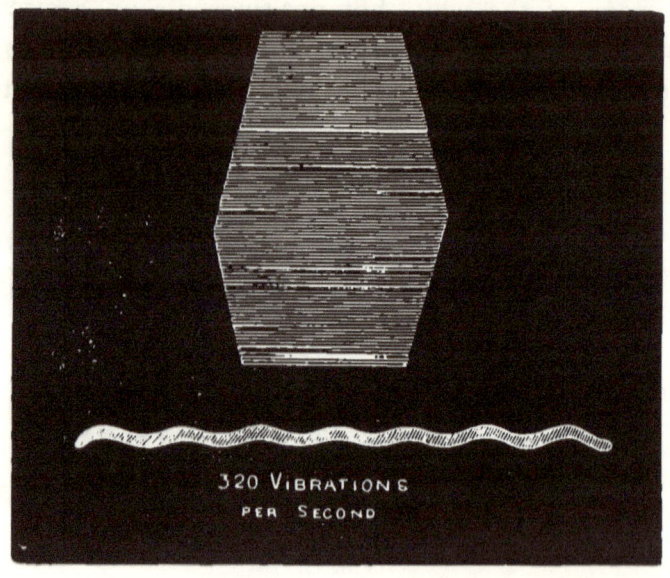

320 VIBRATIONS
PER SECOND

Thornton and Pickard special shutter diagram, with tuning fork vibrations shown. (Taken with slit at diaphragm of the lens.)

FIG. 18.

an image formed of the intersection of the two slits. The tuning fork is set vibrating by a bow, and two more exposures are made, and the vibrations cause a sinuous line to be impressed, each sinuosity being due to a complete vibration of the fork. On development, the diagram the shutter made by its motion across the slit, together with the record of the vibrations, are brought out. An arrangement whereby the two were impressed together was found to be inconvenient and unnecessary, as the period of rotation of the drum remained the same during many experiments when the apparatus remained unaltered. It may be remarked the further away from L_3 that the fork was placed, the more marked, as might be expected, were the sinuosities. When using the camera lens and its diaphragm, the arrangement to secure parallel rays became essential, for evidently if the beam converged through the shutter, the eclipsing of the diaphragm would commence sooner than it would with parallel rays. It became easy by this arrangement to test the shutter's efficiency for any part of the plate that was desired. All that was necessary was to twist the camera B horizontally to such a position that the image of the hole at the end of the collimator fell on its focussing screen at the desired part, and then to proceed as before.

The following is a diagram obtained by this apparatus, and it will be seen how very suggestive it is :—

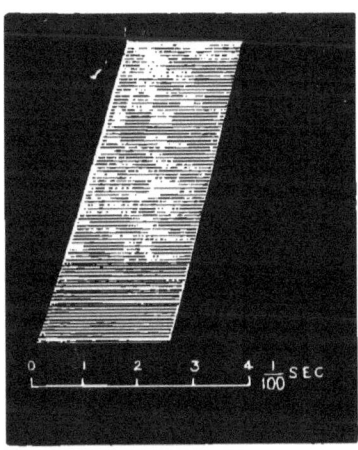

Drop-shutter diagram.
Fig. 19.

It may be asked why the shutter without the lens was

used. For instance, in hand-cameras, would it not have
been better to use its own lens with its stop, as that is
how it is practically used ?   Of course, in such a case
the slit should be at the diaphragm, for that is the place
where it would naturally be of most use.   All that the
slit at the diaphragm would give would be a diagram of
the rapidity of exposure at the centre of the plate, or at
any one desired part by twisting the axis of the camera
lens into the desired direction, whilst what was required
was the rapidity and efficiency at any point of the plate.
The sole exception, of course, is a shutter opening at
the diaphragm, where the whole plate is equally exposed.

Diagrams of several shutters which may be of interest
are shown.   Thornton and Pickard's special shutter,

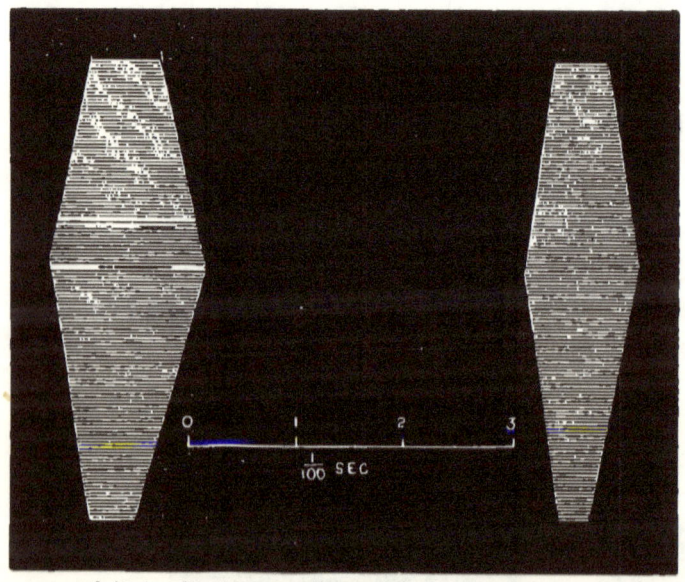

Thornton and Pickard's shutter.   Diagrams taken with slit in the aperture
of the shutter.

Fig. 10.

which is a shutter placed outside of the lens, and

has wings opening and closing centrally, is a good specimen. We have two diagrams on each strip. One was made with the spring wound to give the quickest exposure, and the shutter itself wound to its full extent (Fig. 20). That gives a very short diagram, only some $\frac{1}{30}$ of a second. The second diagram is the same, only the shutter was wound so as only to just close the aperture. In another diagram the spring of the shutter was not wound so tight, but the shutter itself was wound as before. The difference between the first two will be seen. All four have practically the same shape, and the times of opening and closing to and from full aperture have closely the same proportion to

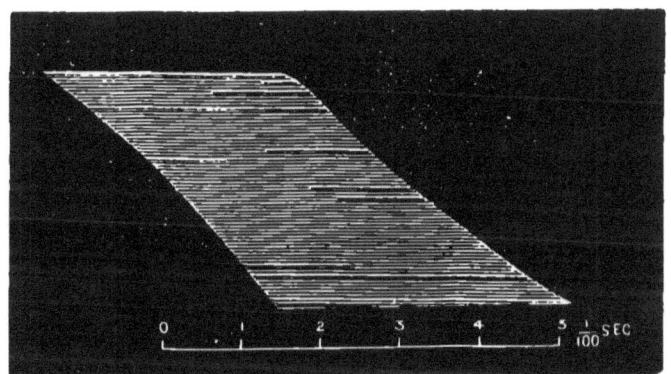

Hawkins' shutter diagram, taken with slit in the aperture of the shutter.

FIG. 21.

the full aperture exposure in all cases. The centre of the plate gets more exposure than the margins, as can be seen by treating the diagram as that of the Hawkins shutter will be immediately.

How the shutter diagrams can be utilized is shown in the annexed figure, which needs, perhaps, a little explanation. S S S S is the diagram of one of Hawkins'

shutters, which is a shutter with an aperture crossing the
back of the lens. Supposing we have a line which is
drawn in section to the same scale, we can, by placing it
sectionally at the distance from the shutter at which it
is proposed to use it, tell what exposure will be given
to any part of the plate, and how much later or earlier
one part will be exposed than another. The scale of
speed in $\frac{1}{100}$ second is attached. The beams, as
refracted, are not shown in the diagram, but some
beams will issue through the stop and come out, as aa,

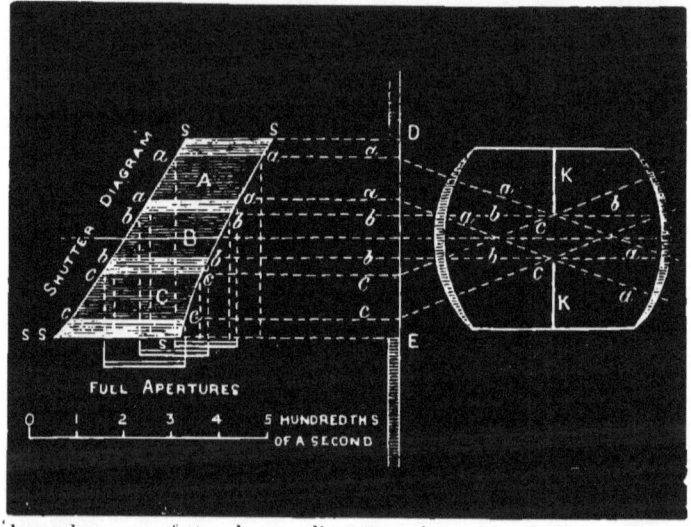

To show what part of the shutter diagram, taken with slit at the aperture of
the shutter, is utilized by rays passing at different angles through the
diaphragm.

FIG. 22.

bb, cc. Where these cut the shutter they are projected
by parallel lines on to the shutter diagram, and the
deeper shaded parts, A B C, show which part of the
shutter will be utilized by such rays. The amount of
full aperture is shown beneath. It will be seen in this
shutter diagram, as indeed in all, that the parts used are

practically bounded by sloping straight lines. These
show the moment when the shutter begins to open and
arrive at full aperture, or when it starts from full aperture and closes. Calculation shows that, with a uniform
motion of a plane across a circle, the exposure is half
that which would be given were the aperture fully open

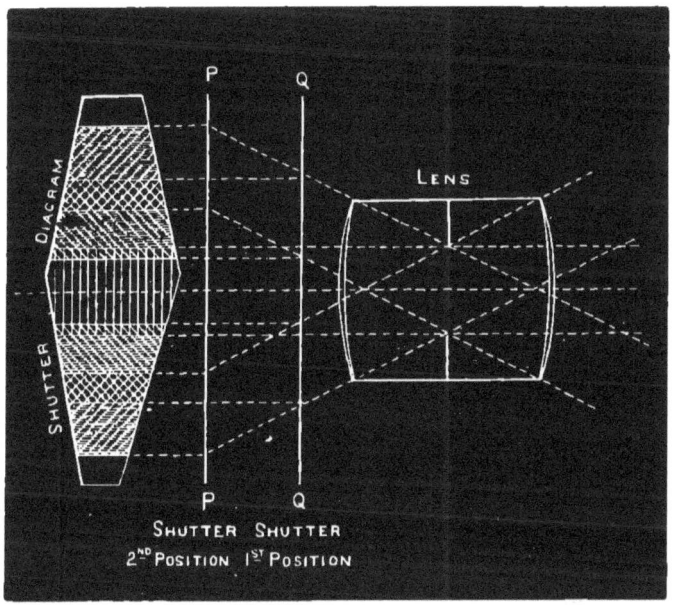

To illustrate the different efficiencies of a shutter when it is fixed at different
distances from the diaphragm.

FIG. 23.

for the same time. (This we have used in a former
chapter, and the reason for it will now be seen.) Now the
practically straight boundary lines show that the motion
of opening and shutting may be considered as uniform.
Under these circumstances it is easy to calculate the actual
exposure, and compare it with the theoretically perfect
exposure : we only have to take the *mean* of the bases of
the little triangles, and add it to the length of the

exposure of full aperture. This has to be compared with the total length of exposure. Thus for the centre rays the bases of the side triangles are, roughly, 9 and 7, and of the full aperture exposure, 24. The exposure in terms of full aperture is thus $8 + 24 = 32$; the theoretical exposure is $9 + 7 + 24 = 40$; the practical exposure is thus ·75, or ¾ that of the theoretical. In this way the exposure at any part of a plate can be worked out, and if the illumination of the field with full aperture is known by other measures, the uniformity or otherwise of exposure can be ascertained. All shutters which move across a lens can be treated in the same way. We can here show the difference that the distance of the shutter from the lens makes in its general efficiency. The diagram of the Thornton and Pickard special shutter (fig. 23) will well illustrate this. It will be seen that if the shutter is in the position Q, it is much more efficient for the marginal rays than it is when in the position P. It may be stated as an axiom that the nearer the shutter is to the diaphragm, the more equally efficient it becomes for the entire plate ; and the further away the less efficient, taking, of course, the efficiency for the central rays as the standard of comparison.

We may here point out that a comparison of the results obtained, by getting the time scale from the syren, and those obtained with the tuning fork, show that either plan is effective. In the one case the time of exposure for the central rays was found to be $\frac{1}{31}$ of a second, and with the other $\frac{1}{33}$, fifteen "turns" being given to the ratchet of the spring in both cases.

The case of a shutter like that of the Key camera, which is a shutter at the diaphragm opening with a

square aperture, has to be differently calculated. In it
we have a space gradually opening from and closing to
the centre. The diagram of this shutter is instructive.
If the lens were square instead of circular, the exposure
for any diaphragm would be given by the cubic content
of a square prism, and of square pyramids terminating

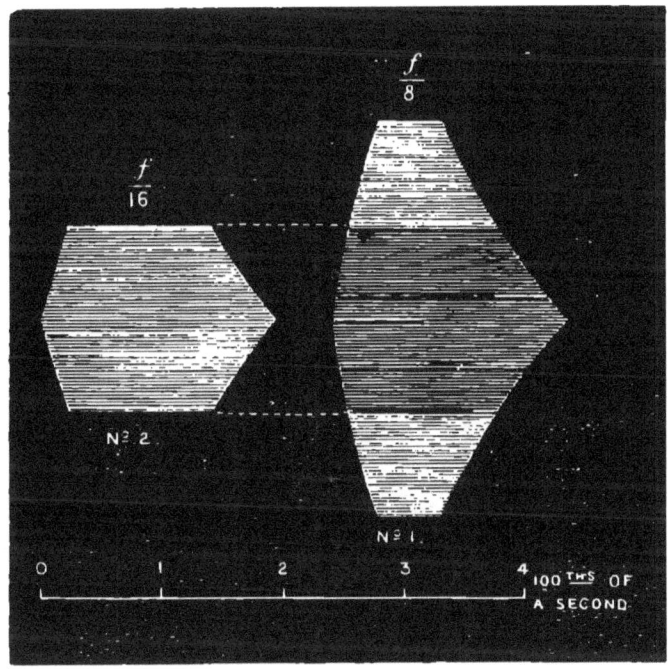

Key shutter diagrams.
No. 1, taken through a diaphragm $f/8$.
No. 2,   ,,   ,,   ,, $f/16$.
FIG. 24.

it. In other words, you have to take the length of full
aperture exposure, and add to it $\frac{1}{3}$ the length of time
elapsing between full aperture and opening and closing.
There is, however, a slight correction to be made for
the circular segments (for the diagram was made with
the slit parallel to one pair of sides of the square

aperture, and placed centrally). When these are made, the efficiency, with a stop $f/8$, is expressed by ·51, and with $f/16$ stop, ·72. *This shows also that you do not gain four times the exposure by using $f/8$ stop when compared with $f/16$ stop, but only about three times*, which is a thing to be remembered. In the same diagram is shown the theoretical exposure with $f/16$ stop, cut out of the $f/8$ diagram, and alongside is the actual diagram made with the latter stop. The two, it will be seen, are identical.

The shutter placed at the diaphragm which should give a nearer approach to a factor of efficiency, unity, is

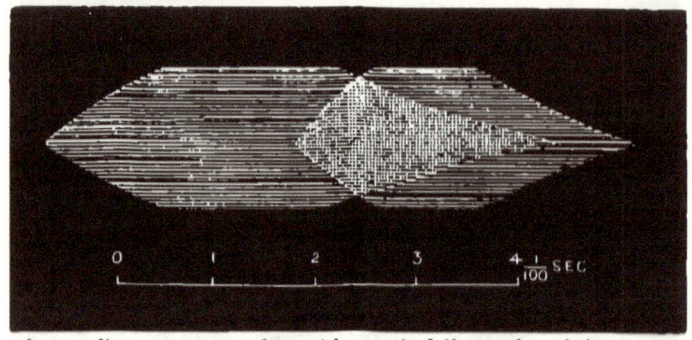

Key shutter diagrams, one taken with nearly full speed, and the second with some " break " on.

FIG. 25.

one made somewhat after the Key fashion, but instead of closing as a square, should close with parallel sides. If the Key shutter were on this principle, and had the same velocities, the speed efficiencies for $f/8$ and $f/16$ stops would be ·64 and ·79. (This kind of shutter we have in one of Adams' hand-cameras. A still nearer approach would be when only one plane crossed the aperture.) Fig. 25 is a double shutter diagram, one being taken with nearly full speed of shutter, and the other with some break on. It will be seen from it that the relation between time of exposure with full aperture and total exposure remains constant.

Where an aperture, of no matter what shape, crosses the lens by a radial motion, the calculations are not quite so simple ; and in such a case it may be advisable to revert to the plan of piercing holes in a card round the aperture, and make each hole draw its own lines, and from such a diagram to make the calculations. There are several lessons to be learnt from these diagrams. In the first place, no shutter has perfect efficiency, and not one, with the exception of the diaphragm shutter, exposes the whole of the plate at the same time. The shutter which works across the back or the front of the lens, in which there are two wings opening at one side and closing at the other, can be made to give fairly equal exposures over every part of the plate, though the start often has the best of it. The shutter which works in front of the lens, closing and opening centrally, gives the margins less exposure than the centre ; but the exposure may be made fairly equable when the lens is shallow—that is, when the shutter is fairly close to the diaphragm. The further off it is, the more the difference in exposure shows. The shutter which works across the lens with only one wing, as in the drop shutter, exposes one margin more than the centre, and the centre than the other margin. Hence it may be usefully employed in landscape work, where the sky can receive slightly less exposure. The bigger the lens, of course the less rapid the shutter. With the diaphragm shutter the smaller the stop the more nearly is unity of efficiency obtained, and the

larger the stop the less efficient it is. A greater
efficiency is obtained by a shutter which moves across
the diaphragm than with one which opens and closes
centrally. The light that may be used for these diagrams
was the electric light, but very satisfactory results have
been obtained by using a strip of magnesium ribbon, or
by a continuous vertical stream of magnesium powder
blown through a spirit flame, after the fashion of Nadar's
lamp.

In reference to these devices for getting a shutter
diagram, it may be stated that there is nothing very
difficult in making a flat plate cross the path of the ray of
light coming through the slit, provided it be sufficiently
long. Equality of motion is not necessary, for it is the
intervals of non-exposure in the plate which tell us the
time of exposure. Nothing else is required. On a
whole-plate, for instance, with a little adroitness, it is
comparatively easy to get a shutter diagram by simply
dropping it across the image. Again, too, it is not
necessary to have any mechanical means of making the
plate or the drum rotate. A good spin given by the
hand suffices to give them sufficient motion for the
purpose, and, as before, the number of intervals of non-
exposure in the developed image suffices to indicate the
time of exposure. This simplifies the apparatus considerably.

We may sum up by saying that the form of shutter
which gives no distortion is that placed at the diaphragm,
and that the worst is that placed close to the plate ; that
no shutter has perfect efficiency, but is nearest to possess-
ing it when a small diaphragm is employed.

CHAPTER VI.

THE question of a lens for instantaneous work has already been touched upon, but we must revert to it again in connection with the instantaneous . shutter which has to be used. From the shutter diagrams which have been made, examples of which have been shown in the previous chapter, it is manifest that the larger the aperture, the less approach to theoretical efficiency a shutter will possess. This is because the time during which the full aperture of the stop is uncovered is much longer with a small aperture than with a large one, always supposing that no change in the extent of the movement of the shutter is made when a stop is changed. The *total time of exposure* will always be the same, whatever stop be used ; and if an object is moving at a rate which shows no perceptible blurring of the image due to that motion when the shutter is set at a certain speed, whatever stop is employed the same want of sharpness of image due to that cause will always obtain. If, however, we "slow" down the shutter, we have at once a tendency for the blurring of the object to be increased. It thus is apparent that it is better to use a larger stop to obtain proper exposure than it is to

E

slow down the shutter. provided, of course, the lens covers properly when the larger aperture is employed. If a lens has been critically tried, as explained in a previous chapter, we can tell what is the limit to which we may enlarge the aperture without losing definition due to the imperfections of the lens, and we can safely increase the total exposure by using a stop up to that aperture, but not further. When more exposure is required than this will give, we must put the break on the shutter and slow down its speed. With some lenses which are made with Jena glass, we can use an aperture of about $f/6$—that is, $\frac{1}{6}$ of the focal length—without any loss worth mentioning in the definition of the field ; and with such a lens it may safely be said that, as a rule, the shutter should not be slowed, for, if it has to be, it is pretty certain the conditions are such that instantaneous photography is difficult.

The point now presents itself as to what speed the shutter should be confined. There are very few shutters extant which give an exposure of the $\frac{1}{1000}$ of a second ; the $\frac{1}{10}$ of a second is much more common. As a rule, for distant views with figures not too close, the $\frac{1}{20}$ of a second is the shortest exposure that is absolutely necessary, whilst many objects need not have less than $\frac{1}{10}$ of a second, such objects being breaking waves, and ordinary landscapes. even with trees blowing about, and so on. For rapidly moving objects, if the $\frac{1}{1000}$ of a second can be secured, so much the better, and a large stop must be used with a good light. This shows that there is a variation allowable, even with the shutter, and in certain conditions of weather it is a distinct advantage to have the use of the slower shutter, and also the larger stop ;

but we would much prefer to use a quick speed of
shutter with a large stop, than a less rapid speed with
a smaller stop. For instantaneous work the iris diaphragm to a lens is an admirable adjunct, for it is
distinctly an encouragement for the photographer to
alter the stop instead of the rapidity of the shutter.
The insertion of a Waterhouse diaphragm takes time,
and of all things perhaps in instantaneous photography
time is the most precious, and this the photographer
often gains by using the break to the shutter, rather
than by altering the stop. The iris diaphragm is an
old invention, but if the writer had to name a re-invention
which deserves special praise, it is that of this handy
kind of diaphragm. To sum up, regarding lens, diaphragm, and shutter, we may say that a lens which can
work with a flat field and sharp with a stop $f/6$, which
has an iris diaphragm, and a shutter which closes
in the $\frac{1}{70}$th of a second, are what we should look
for in instantaneous work. A single lens is sometimes recommended, but its drawback is the distortion
of straight lines.   Though not quite useless for
architectural work, or for views in which buildings are
to be found, yet it is unsatisfactory, and can rarely be
used with a stop so large as that with which a doublet
can be used. It gives a brighter image because it has
fewer reflecting surfaces; but the brightness rarely
exceeds by more than ten per cent. that of a good
colourless doublet lens; for, as stated, the thickness of
glass through which light passes has but little to do
with the falling off of the intensity.   The first thin
layer, which must be alike in both single and doublet
lens, is that which has most effect. A striking example

of this was given by Professor Boys, who showed that
the difference in chemical action on a plate when
shielded by microscopic glass, or by glass of ordinary
thickness, was practically the same in both cases. It
will be judged that the shutter which we most prefer
is between the lenses, and this naturally confines our
choice to some few which are specially adapted for it.
We may mention the shutter supplied by the Platinotype
Company with their Key camera, and the latest Furnel
shutter, as good types of diaphragm shutters; whilst for
those working outside the lens we have many. Amongst
the very best, as giving a good diagram, we may mention the Thornton-Pickard shutter. It may be taken
as a maxim that the less complicated the shutter is,
the more satisfactory it will be in the long run. The
fewer things there are to get out of order the better,
and a simple shutter is always more easy to repair, and
is less expensive to renew. For instantaneous work
that is carried out in a camera fastened to a camera-
stand the drop-shutter is very satisfactory when it is
light, but care must be taken that it does not shake the
camera in the act of letting off. This liability to shake
is much less with shutters to which a pneumatic
arrangement is attached, for reasons which will be
obvious. With a hand-camera a shutter of this
description is almost inadmissible, for it is apt to come
in contact with the hands when the catch is released.
The pneumatic principle of release here requires a third
hand, or a substitute for such a hand, and therefore the
method of releasing by hand must be resorted to,
though in some cases the mouth may be used to inflate
the teat which effects the release.

CHAPTER VII.

A QUESTION is very often asked as to what plates should be used in instantaneous photography. There are certain essential characteristics which may be mentioned without giving any brand a gratuitous advertisement. A plate for instantaneous work should not be starved in emulsion, but it should be fairly dense when looking through it. Such being the case, one may expect that of necessity the plates will not always be the cheapest in the market, for if they were sold at the lowest price, the amount of material that is employed would run the profits very fine. If it be thinly coated there is not much latitude in exposure, and for this kind of work it is essential that there should be ; for although a plate has some one exposure which, with a certain mode of development, is probably the best, yet deviation from this exposure has to be allowed for, and this is secured by having a good thickness of film. It should also be as rapid as possible, and the method of arriving at a conclusion regarding the rapidity will be touched on presently.

The plate should also be evenly coated, which implies that, amongst other things, the glass should be as flat as can be obtained. The glass used for ordinary plates is anything but uniformly flat, and if the best work is to be carried out with ordinary photography, this flatness should be secured. It need scarcely be said that the plate should be free from spots which refuse to develop, or from spots which develop too much ; in other words, it should be as perfect as possible, and as rapid as possible. It may further be remarked—and this applies to all kinds of photography—that the methods very often adopted for separating plates from each other are, in many cases, inadequate. There is nothing more annoying than to find, on an otherwise perfect negative, marks due to the rubbing together of the sensitive surfaces of two plates. If the plates were really flat, this could not occur, since the strips of that paper forming the separation would be sufficient to prevent it. One maker, at least, has adopted the plan of cutting through the glass of a double-sized plate without breaking the gelatine film, and folding the two face to face. This is an excellent plan, since the films are immovable, and even when the glass is not quite flat, no rubbing marks are found. Another disadvantage of separating plates by edgings of thick paper is, that they may often show markings where the paper has been in contact with these. Sometimes these parts are fogged, and sometimes seem as if sensitiveness had been lost. Some makers pack with thin paper between the surfaces, and when such paper is free from con- tamination it answers well ; but in this case the maker is very much in the hands of the paper-maker. If plates or films are not intended to be kept long, this plan will answer, however, when care in the selection of the paper has been exercised. As a rule, if one plate in a box shows spots, the others will also have this defect. A very crucial test is to expose a plate to naked candle light for a period sufficiently long to cause the surface to blacken under development. Any trace of opaque or insensitive spots will be at once seen, and if they are numerous, or of a pronounced character, beware of the remainder! One defect that is now rarely met with is incorrectness in cutting the plates to the proper size. There is nothing much more annoying than this, and it is a defect for which the plate-maker is absolutely responsible.

Now as to the rapidity of a plate. It is not intended to enter into the methods which a plate-maker may adopt for the purpose of measuring it; more especially as there is more than a suspicion that the comparative rapidities of a plate may alter according to the intensity of the light employed. The following plan will, however, give a very good idea of how the rapidity of a plate can be guaged. Take a quarter-plate, say of medium rapidity, but giving good density, and expose a strip of it to an ordinary paraffin candle, at a distance of six feet, for five seconds, an adjoining strip for ten, another for twenty, and so on, each time doubling till an exposure of 640 seconds has been arrived at (a strip of the plate should remain unexposed). Now develop, and we have a scale of different transparencies. In a case in point, the following were the transparencies of the different strips, calling 0 sec., 100; 5 sec., 83·5; 10 sec., 65; 20 sec., 40; 40 sec., 24; 80 sec., 10·5; 160 sec., 5; 320 sec., 2·7; 640 sec., 1·5. If we place this scale of transparency in contact with the plate to be tried in the dark slide in the camera, using the lens with an aperture of $f/8$, or whatever aperture it is proposed to employ, and, with the shutter set at its usual rapidity, give an exposure on a bright day to the reflection of the sun from white paper, or to an evenly-lighted sky, an image of the scale of shade will be produced. If the plate is sufficiently rapid to be impressed by the light coming through the densest strip, such as given above, it may be taken that the plate is fit for the purpose of instantaneous photography. Two or three plates may be tried at the same time, by cutting them into strips, and giving an exposure together.

On a cloudy day, or when there is a blue sky, the test will be still more exacting ; but if a plate which is known to be fit for the work be exposed with that under trial, a very good notion of the comparative rapidities can be obtained. It is better, as said before, to use daylight if possible, than any artificial light in these trials. It must further be recollected that the visual brightness of the image seen on the focussing screen by no means represents the true photographic brightness. The ground glass itself allows a great deal of the light to pass through it, and only a percentage forms the image on the screen. If the true brightness has to be seen, it should be viewed on an opaque white screen, from which all light except that of the image itself is excluded, when at once the difference will be manifested. Further, it must be recollected that the photographic is very different to the visual value of daylight. Sunlight is said to have a visual illuminating power of 5,000 candles if they could all be placed at one foot's distance from a white screen. If this be so, it has a photographic value of 100,000 candles at the same distance. So, in order to estimate visually the photographic value of the camera image with a stop $f/8$ in comparison with one formed by candle-light, it would be necessary to insert a stop about $f/1\cdot8$ to give it ; or, again, the brightness of an image with $f/8$ will be visually about the photographic brightness of an image when using $f/36$.

CHAPTER VIII.

THE question next arises as to when an instantaneous photograph can be taken. This point has, in some measure, already been referred to before. The writer believes that, under moderate conditions as to weather, there is no day at any time of year, with a rapid plate, on which an instantaneous photograph of a fairly open landscape may not be taken between the hours of nine in the morning and three in the afternoon by using a stop of $f_{,}8$, with a shutter which can give the one-tenth of a second's exposure. On a bright day in summer the stop that can be used is often as small as $f/22$, and even $f/32$, with an exposure of one-fiftieth of a second. This means, on the old system of calculation, supposing $f/22$ be used in summer, that, with equally well-exposed negatives, the light (say in December) is forty times less photographically intense than in July, or, if $f/16$ is used, ten times less intense. This is not far from the truth. As an example, it may be stated that, with one of the most rapid plates in the market, early in December, about 11 a.m. on a cloudy day, with occasional gleams of sunshine, perfectly exposed negatives of near oak-trees, with old brown foliage on them, in Richmond Park, were obtained under the circumstances described. The same trees were taken in the previous July with $f/16$, about 10 a.m., the shutter set to give one-fiftieth second, and the exposure was more than sufficient, although the shadows were very heavy. As a rule, the amateur puts away his photographic kit for instantaneous work as soon as the short days commence. This is a mistake, for effects can often be obtained at such a time, owing to the low altitude of the sun, which cannot be found on days which are long. Abroad, particularly at high altitudes, where the air is clearer and the sun brighter, views can be obtained later in the day (or earlier) than at home ; for instance, with $f/8$ and one-twentieth of a second exposure, good views in fairly wide streets of Rome have been obtained in January up to 3·45 p.m. The writer has obtained in the middle of February views in the city (London) which have been fully exposed. It cannot, however, be too much insisted upon that, for such purposes, really rapid plates should be employed. It must not, however, be considered that *any* view can be taken under these circumstances. For instance, a path through a wood or a narrow street is impracticable very often under apparently favourable conditions. Let us consider the case of the narrow street view. It is highly improbable that much sun can reach it even in summer, and much less so in the winter. The illumination is, therefore, that due to the sky. Now, though the light from the whole sky—or, say, from half the sky—may be sufficient to illuminate a wall so as to impress the photographic plate, yet if we have but a small fraction of the sky-light available, as is the case in such a street view, it is manifest that the illumination must be deficient, and no amount of "coaxing" in development will give a satisfactory picture.

The writer has seen amateurs, and some who ought to know better, go into a gallery wainscoated with fairly dark oak, and give an instantaneous exposure to obtain a negative. Seemingly to such, if an apparatus is labelled as suitable for instantaneous work, any and every view is to be taken with a shutter. One trait in the general character of a young photographer is his credulity. He has implicit faith in the use and meaning of words, but forgets that photographic goods—like the pedlar's razors—are often made to sell.

In calculating the stop to use and the exposure to give, the photographer should pay attention to several things before making his final determination. He should see how much sky, for instance, is available for illuminating the darkest part of his picture ; also whether the local colour is a good one for reflecting photographic light. Thus, a red brick wall is not so good as a grey stone wall, for obvious reasons ; or the dark green foliage of, say, a fir-tree, not so fit for reflecting the necessary light as the paler green of an elm, and so on. He should determine to expose, as far as possible or practicable, for the deep shadows, so as to get something in them beyond general transparency. It may be noted here that, in any close views, there is scarcely any probability of over-exposing when a shutter is employed, the dark shadows being usually very black through want of atmosphere between the lens and the object. For open views this is, however, by no means the case. There is always a certain amount of "sky" present between the lens and the object, and in the photograph this sky is impressed. The word sky is used here advisedly. The blue light in the sky is caused by small floating particles in the atmosphere which scatter more of the blue than of the yellow and red rays of the spectrum—that is, these last are more transmitted, whilst the first go to form the blue of the sky. These particles are particularly present near the surface of the ground, and they scatter and reflect the light similarly to those particles which are above us.

Over-exposure on a thinly-coated plate means a flat image, which only intensification subsequently can render possible for printing purposes. It should also be remembered that white objects in the foreground (say, a white road) are difficult to deal with, but they are useful for reflecting light into the deeper shadows. When the sun is high in a cloudless sky it is well-nigh impossible to get a good landscape view ; the shadows are too short and too black to deal with successfully under any circumstances, and especially for instantaneous work. It is impossible to fix any altitude for the sun with which not to work, for so much depends upon the character of the sky. If there be fleecy clouds about, which act as reflectors of a good deal of the sunlight, views may be taken which should not be attempted if the sky were clear. On a bright summer's day it is not a bad plan to take a siesta before noon, have lunch, and afterwards smoke a quiet pipe, and then begin serious work. By this time the sun will have sunk to a reasonable altitude, and the hard work of the day will commence. On a grey day the camera may be at work without any such pleasant interval, and the effects will be almost as pleasing—or as little pleasing—at one time as at another.

When the sun is only about twenty-five degrees above the horizon, exposures will have to be prolonged. The stop should be changed to a larger one then, and, as sunset approaches, one still larger should be inserted; and as a last resort, the shutter should be "slowed," as already explained. Not many photographers at home are accustomed to see sunrises in summer, but those who do should follow the same rules as for sunset work. It is often said that the light is better at sunrise than at sunset. This is so in some cases, but as often the reverse. If the sun rises or sets very red, the light will be worse than if it sets orange or yellow.

CHAPTER IX.

THE writer has recently been using orthochromatic plates with a screen for instantaneous views, and has come to the conclusion that under certain conditions, and for some purposes, they are at an advantage over the ordinary sensitive plate. In the market there are several brands of orthochromatic plates—isochromatic, they are sometimes called—all of which have a certain amount of sensitiveness to certain colours by which the ordinary plate is almost unaffected. These orthochromatic plates may be classed into two kinds, some which are sensitive to the yellow and green rays (besides the blue and the violet), and the others which are sensitive to red and yellow (besides the blue and the violet). If we examine a landscape through an orange glass we shall find that the blue sky appears darker than it is in reality, whilst the faintest white clouds, which we hardly distinguish when viewed without the glass, become well-marked objects. The green of foliage and grass is also rendered yellower, whilst a red brick house appears unchanged. These effects are produced by reason of the orange glass cutting off the violet and a large amount of the blue rays which exist in the light. Evidently, in

order to benefit by this absorption of those rays which
are principally active in ordinary photography, we must
have a plate which is sensitive to the colours transmitted.
Both kinds of orthochromatic plates will answer this
purpose, though, of course, they will require longer
exposure when such a screen is employed in conjunction
with the lens. With the orange glass employed the
writer found that an exposnre twelve times more prolonged was required than that for the same plate when
no screen was employed.

The plates employed were sensitive to yellow and
green, as well as to the blue. Using a stop of $f/16$ it
was found that an ordinary exposure, without the yellow
glass, was about the $\frac{1}{25}$th of a second in March on a
fairly open view. The lens employed was such that
most perfect definition could be obtained when $f/5·6$
was employed over the whole of a quarter-plate. Now
this stop means that about eight times more light is
admitted to a plate. If the shutter used had the
same efficiency with $f/5·6$ that it had with $f/16$, it is
evident that the speed might have been reduced to
$\frac{1}{10}$th of a second to get proper exposure with the yellow
glass inserted. As a matter of fact, it is not quite so
efficient, so the shutter was slowed down till it gave an
exposure of $\frac{1}{10}$th of a second. When this was done an
exposure through the orange glass with an aperture $f/5·6$
was found ample. In summer weather the speed may
be diminished to the $\frac{1}{25}$th of a second, and satisfactory
pictures can be got.

The explanation of the altered appearance of the sky
when viewed through the orange glass may be given
here.

In sky-light there are proportionally many more blue and violet rays for an equal intensity of light than there are in sunlight. Now clouds are simply reflectors of sunlight when they are seen as white. It can therefore be very readily seen that as the orange glass cuts off nearly all blue and violet rays from every kind of light, it will leave the sky apparently much darker than it does the clouds, and as the residual light affects the plate, it will be affected in closely the same proportion as the brightness which the two seem to be to the eye. If no screen be used, the larger proportion of blue light in the sky will make it relatively more photographically actinic than the clouds, and hence there may be little or no distinction between the two.

Discretion must be used in choosing the glass. There are various tints of orange, and even a light yellow glass is often effective, particularly when the sun gets low. A light yellow glass will only prolong the exposure three or four times, and is very suitable for afternoon views. In choosing the glass, care must be taken that it is optically flat. If the image of a window be viewed on the surfaces of the glass, and the window bars remain undistorted when the glass is turned in every direction, it may be assumed that the glass is sufficiently flat for the purpose.

Another plan is to place a piece of white card at a distance of, say, five feet from the glass, and reflect a beam of sunlight (not transmitted through a window pane) on to it. If the glass is flat, the patch of sunlight on the card should be of about the same size as the glass itself, and show no striæ or markings. It may happen that a part will appear to be without any flaws, judging

F

by the patch of light on the card, and this part may be used, if sufficiently large, to cover the lens. "Worked" glass can be obtained, but it is expensive, and usually some small area in the ordinary coloured glass may be found which will be sufficiently plane as judged by either of the above methods.

When a piece is chosen, it should be placed *in situ* (the writer prefers it behind rather than in front of the lens), and the image of a distant landscape be examined. A newspaper may be substituted for the landscape if more convenient. The image should be as sharp with the glass as without it.

With the lens the writer used, the screen could not be placed at the diaphragm, as there was no room for it ; but with some lenses, for the usual metal stop one of cardboard may be cut out, and picked thin microscopic glass be coated with collodion in which aurantia has been dissolved, and placed in the aperture so cut. There seems to be a future for instantaneous orthochromatic photography on the lines indicated above.

CHAPTER X.

DEVELOPMENT of the picture is the next point we have to consider, and this is by no means unimportant. One thing has to be recollected, and this is, that a very rapid plate is very frequently, *but not always*, difficult to develop with bare shadows. We may first of all consider what we really have to develop compared with an ordinary artificial light. Measuring the camera image with a stop $f/8$ by means of an amyl-acetate lamp, it will be found that the sky has a value varying from five of these units on a grey day, to three times that value on a really bright day, and that the highest light, such as brilliantly illuminated clouds, is again three or four times brighter; whilst the deepest shadow that is required to be shown has a value of about $\frac{1}{30}$ of the same unit. Roughly speaking, it may be said, then, that the highest light on bright days is about 250 times brighter than that of the deepest shadow.

This has to be rendered on a print with a comparative brightness of about 30 to 1, this being somewhere about that of white paper to platinum black as found in a platinum print. It is quite evident, then, that if it were possible in the negative—which it is not—to have a difference between the transparency of the deposit given by the highest light used, and the deepest shadows of 250 and 1, and all the intervening gradations in proper relation, that by far the largest part of the print would either show black with gradations in the whites, or whites with gradation in the shadows. What we have to do is to reduce the gradation of the negative as far as possible proportionally. This means that the image must be full of detail throughout, and at the same time have the highest light shown as white, and the deepest shadows as black. This is a problem which requires careful attention, and depends on two factors : 1st, the plate used ; 2nd, the method of development, and kind of developer. Now the quicker the plate in a bright light, the less steep is the gradation ; that is, if a moderately quick plate allows 50 per cent. of light to pass with an exposure to a certain intensity of light, and 5 per cent. to pass with another, then with a quick plate this ratio will be much less for exposure to the same relative intensities of light. A quick plate, then, will be much more capable of giving the necessary gradation required. One winter lately, at Rome, the writer exposed two brands of plates, both supposed to have the same rapidity, on the same subject. With the one, the highest light to the deepest shadows were harmonious, and the details in all parts were shown. With the other, though the same detail was to be found, it was not printable in both the shadows and in the high-lights ; a careful measurement of the transparencies of the plates when exposed in artificial and in daylight showed that for camera images the first was really more

sensitive than the second, though this was not to be dis-
covered by the artificial light. It is not an unfrequent
complaint that is made, that plates which give a brilliant
image when tested by the latter light, will often give a
feeble image in the camera which nothing seems to
avert. Forcing up density will generally induce fog,
and this is to be avoided.

Now what is the development to be adopted? Per-
sonally, the writer prefers a thin image, full of detail,
and which can be intensified as one may desire; and
this plan is one which he adopts. For this reason
pyrogallic acid and ammonia development are avoided,
for though the image may appear to be thin, its
appearance may be deceitful, for if it have that
green tint which is so often characteristic of this
development, it will often be too hard to give a soft and
delicate print, though if it were a jet black deposit, it
would be too thin. A great point is to avoid fog,
and notwithstanding what is said to the contrary, it
is impossible to obtain this without a fair quantity of
alkaline bromide in the developer, and the more energetic
the developer, the more bromide there will be required.
One thing more, however, must be remembered, which is,
that a plate made with a hard gelatine, or a plate in which
the proportion of sensitive salt is small compared with
that of the gelatine enclosing it, will require less bromide
than if the gelatine is soft, or if the sensitive salt is
abundant. With this in view, the amount of bromide
must be regulated. In most formulæ for the new
developers, such as eikonogen and metol, it is told us
that no bromide is required. This is perfectly true with
some plates, but if others are developed without it, fog

inevitably will result. For our own part, we like either of these two named developers for the purpose in view, for the deposit is black, and the visual and photographic transparency of the different parts are practically identical, so that one is able to judge by the eye of what one may expect in a print. Besides this advantage, they are also easy to work, and retain their developing powers for some time after they are prepared.

CHAPTER XI.

In developing rapid plates, care should be taken to avoid an over strong light from striking on them, even though it be of what is considered a safe colour. The writer uses a portable lantern in a darkened room, the diagram of which is taken from "Instruction in Photography." It was first introduced by Mr. G. S. Edwards in a cylindrical form, but it is more convenient when modified to the following shape.

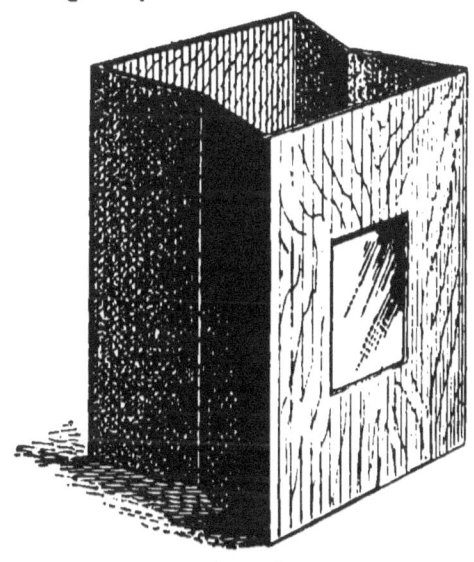

Fig. 26.

A sheet of canary paper is laid upon a sheet of orange paper, and the two sides are gummed together that if

spread out it would be a cylinder open top and bottom.
It is then folded into four creases, and two opposite
ones again creased in the middle. When placed on the
table it presents the form as shown in fig. 26. An
ordinary bedroom candlestick can be placed inside.
The top is covered with a shade, as shown in fig. 27,

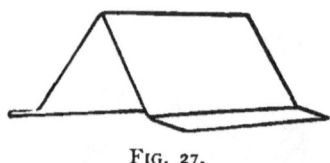

FIG. 27.

to screen the light from the ceiling. It is simply a
folded quarter-sheet of thick canary paper. This lantern
folds up perfectly flat in its creases, and can be placed
in a drawer, or at the bottom of the portmanteau. A
small window giving a brighter light can be made in one
side of the lantern by cutting out the orange paper, the
light thus passing only through the canary paper. In
using this lantern the window should be turned away
from the dish in which development takes place, the
main illumination being by the orange light coming
through both papers. When daylight is used, the
window is best blocked out with opaque paper, except
a couple of panes, and these should be taken out, and
stained red glass inserted in their place. These should
be covered either with orange paper or with canary
paper. It must never be forgotten that plates are only
insensitive to this kind of light when the exposure to it
is not prolonged. To test the truth of this assertion a
piece of a plate may be covered up, and the remainder
exposed for, say, ten minutes to the light. On development the covered-up portion will remain bright,

whilst the other portion will show signs of exposure. For this reason it is advisable to cover up the dish during development by a piece of card. The card can be removed from time to time to watch the progress of the image, and when it is well out this protection may be thrown aside, for a plate in which development has proceeded some way becomes much less sensitive than before the developer has been applied. Looking through a negative is but little guide to the true opacity of the image, as it is so loaded with unaltered silver bromide.

A word or two of warning must be given as to the colour of the light employed. With some plates the canary paper is sufficient protection, but with others, in which a certain amount of iodide is mixed with the bromide, it is dangerous. Again, too, the orange paper varies in hue. There is one which is redder than other brands. When examined by the spectroscope it is found that some blue rays pass through it. If the cover of this book be taken as a sample of the orange paper used, it will be found to be safe in every respect.

For orthochromatic plates even such a light, unless used judiciously, is insecure, since they are sensitive to the colour transmitted through orange and yellow. For those plates which are only sensitive to the yellow, a combination of ruby glass and canary medium may be taken as sufficiently safe, if used at a respectful distance. The safest light is, however, a green light, such as recommended by the writer in 1880 for use with his red sensitive emulsion. If a lantern be glazed with a signal green glass and a bottle green glass, the light transmitted will scarcely affect the orthochromatic plates sensitive to either the red or the yellow, since it lies in that part of the spectrum which has a minimum effect on them.

The light of a candle filtered through such glasses is very feeble, and plates can be developed in it free from fog if the precaution of covering the dish is not neglected. With plates such as these daylight is too strong, unless it be so subdued that it is really visually feebler than artificial light.

As an antithesis to this it may be said that any plate may be developed in naked candle light, and yet be free from fog, if the candle be placed far enough off, and it be so arranged that the light is not reflected from a white ceiling or light-coloured walls. The most rapid plate, exposed for ten seconds to a naked candle forty feet off, and fully shining on it, shows no signs of exposure. A plate might be exposed to this light during transferrence to the developing dish, and whilst it is being covered with the developer, and still show no signs of fog if it be covered up during the initial stage of development. The great point is for a photographer to know what he can and what he can't do, and this is one of the things that he should know, as it may be of use to him.

It is to be remembered that the same kind of light in which development may take place should be employed for changing the plates.

CHAPTER XII.

THE predilection of the writer, which was stated at the end of Chapter X., as to the developer to use, must not bias the readers, for certainly other workers obtain results with pyrogallic acid which leave nothing to be desired. Formulæ which are recommended are therefore given. The formula which, perhaps, is able to bring out most detail is that recommended originally by the late Col. Stuart Wortley. By his plan the plate is first soaked for a couple of minutes in dilute ammonia, and then the bromide and pyrogallic acid are added subsequently, little by little, till proper density is obtained.

The formula stands thus—

No. 1.

Ammonia	1 drachm
Water	9 drachms

No. 2.
Pyrogallic acid (dry).

No. 3.
Sulphite of soda (a saturated solution).

No. 4.

Potassium bromide	20 grains
Water	1 ounce

One drachm of No. 1 is mixed with 2 ounces of water, and the plate is flooded with this till the film is saturated with it; 1 drachm of No. 4, 1 drachm of No. 3, with 1½ grains of No. 2, are placed in the developing glass. The ammonia is poured back again, and the mixed developer is applied. The development is continued till the image appears well at the back of the plate, or if it lags, more of Nos. 2, 3, and 4 are added till this result is obtained. With this development it is well to use alum, as the film is apt to get loose on the glass. After washing, it is therefore placed in a 7 or 8 per cent. solution of alum. It is again well washed, when it is placed in the usual fixing bath—

| Hyposulphite of soda | .. | .. | 1 ounce |
| Water | .. .. | .. | .. 6 ounces |

It is again thoroughly washed, and the density examined. If too weak, it may be at once intensified by one or other of the methods which are at present extant (see next Chapter).

Two drachms of a 10 per cent. solution (50 grains of the salt to 1 ounce of water) of carbonate of soda may be substituted for the drachm of No. 1, as given above. In this case we have an alkaline solution, which is not liable to lose strength through evaporation. Many photographers like this better than the ammonia on this account.

Perhaps the developer which, when used as a "one-fluid" developer, brings out more detail in a shorter time than any other, is the metol developer, and this can be employed in nearly every case where exposure within proper limits is employed. It is energetic and

quick acting, but if it errs at all, it errs in not giving
quite enough density.

It should be made as follows :—

Metol	8 grains
Sulphite soda	50 ,,
Carbonate of soda..	50 ,,
Bromide of potassium	½ grain
Water	2 ounces

This developer is very rapid in its initial action, and the
image is a phantom one at first. In case it appears too
rapidly, the action should be stopped by washing the
plate, and applying a (20 grains to the ounce of water)
solution of bromide of potassium. Density may be
obtained by again washing, and applying a solution of
pyrogallic acid (3 grains to the ounce of water), and
developing as usual. There will be just sufficient alkali
left in the film to allow a reduction of silver on those
parts on which a deposit had taken place, this allowing
good density to be attained.

A very favourite developer with the writer is the amidol.
The image appears very rapidly at first, and gradually
obtains density. It is a mistake to hurry in development. The image should appear well at the back of
the plate if printing density is to be obtained. It can
be made as follows :—

Amidol	5 grains
Sodium sulphite	40 ,,
Potassium bromide	1 grain
Water	2 ounces

This solution will keep a few days, but is most energetic
when used fresh. Both this and the metol may be used

for a good number of plates ; 6 oz. of either should develop twenty-four quarter-plates, using the fresh solution for those which were suspected of being barely exposed sufficiently.

Before development is commenced the plate should be thoroughly brushed over with a soft *dry* brush. (The word dry is italicized because so often the brush is left carelessly about.) Before the plate is taken out of the slide and put into the dish, the developing solution should be ready at hand to prevent an access of light to it. The solution should be evenly applied, and cover the plate at once. If it stop in its flow there will be a great probability of markings showing on the finished negatives. There are many kinds of dishes in the market at the present time. There are none which are better than the celluloid for travelling, though, for some work, good flat white dishes about 1¼ inches in depth are to be preferred for cleanliness sake. It is always as well to avoid putting the fingers in the developer if possible, and if the end of an ordinary wooden match be cut to a wedge shape, this will lift the plate out of the solution readily, when it can be seized by the hands and examined as required. A similar one may be used for the fixing bath, but the same one should not be used for the developing solution as well as the fixing solution, for hyposulphite of soda, even in small quantities, is not a desirable addition to most developers.

CHAPTER XIII.

THE most perfect intensification is carried out by the plan which was introduced by Mr. Chapman Jones, but in the writer's experience it has to be carefully carried out, or success will be wanting.

In the first place, all hyposulphite must be got rid of. If the washing be not complete, steps must be taken to remove any trace of it. The writer himself prefers a solution of hydroxyl, since it readily attacks hyposulphite, without effecting any decomposition of the silver. If a solution of hydroxyl be obtained it may be diluted— 20 parts to 1—and the plate immersed in it for a quarter of an hour. Failing this, another application of the alum bath may be given, or a very dilute solution (1 in 200) of hydrochloric acid. This last will effectually remove the hyposulphite. The plate is then washed, and immersed in a saturated solution of mercuric chloride (bichloride of mercury), to each ounce of which a drop of strong hydrochloric acid has been added, until the whole of the silver is converted into a white substance, which is a double chloride of mercury and silver. The acid prevents the formation of a compound which is prejudicial in subsequent operations. The film is next thoroughly washed. The washing, if possible, should take place in running water, and continue for a quarter of an hour, or until the white surface begins to get a little brown from the alkaline carbonates which are to be found in most waters. It is not a bad plan, when many negatives have to be washed, to make a shallow trough just the width of the plate, and which will hold half-a-dozen at a time. The trough is filled with the plates, and placed at a gentle slope under the water supply. The stream of water will thus pass over each negative in succession, and the whole number will be washed at one time. When the washing is complete the plates are immersed in a solution of ferrous oxalate, which is prepared as follows :—

A.

Ferrous sulphate   ..   A saturated solution.

B.

Potassium oxalate   ..   A saturated solution.

One part of A is poured into 4 parts of B, and the resulting red liquid is ferrous oxalate in solution mixed with potassic sulphate, an inert body as far as the developer is concerned. This is applied to the bleached plate in ordinary daylight, and after some considerable time the white film at its upper surface becomes black, and finally the same hue is taken by the particles next the back of the plate. When this occurs the intensification is complete. The plate may then be washed and dried ; but with most waters, if this be done without any intermediate bath, the plate takes markings somewhat like watered silk, due to the formation of insoluble oxalate of lime caused by the decomposition of the potassium oxalate by the carbonate of lime in the water. The writer's practice is to soak the plate for some five minutes, after washing, in dilute hydrochloric or citric acid, which decomposes this oxalate of lime, when it may be rinsed well, and set up to dry. A couple of washes of distilled water after bleaching, and after the application of the ferrous oxalate, will answer as well as the above acid solution. If any hyposulphite have been left in the film, yellow stains are liable to appear in what should be the transparent parts, and the same happens if the mercuric chloride which is not in combination with the silver has failed to be removed.

This method of intensification is such as to about double the visual opacity of the film for the half-tones, and it has the advantage that it may be repeated till any desired density is arrived at.

The other method of intensification is by means of cyanide of silver following on the bleaching by chloride of mercury. It may be remarked that for bleaching for this last method, some prefer to employ mercuric bromide. This is obtained by mixing with the mercuric chloride, potassium bromide, mercuric bromide and potassium chloride being formed.

The formula for bleaching is as follows :—

Mercuric chloride..	..	..	100 grains
Potassium bromide	..	..	100 ,,
Water	.. .. ..	..	10 ounces

And for blackening the deposit :—

| Nitrate of silver .. | .. | .. | 100 grains |
| Water | .. .. .. | .. | 10 ounces |

To this silver solution is added cyanide of potassium

G

(which is a deadly poison) in sufficient quantity to very nearly but not quite dissolve the cyanide of silver first formed.

It is convenient to make a solution of 100 grains of cyanide of potassium to the ounce of water, and add it gradually till this end is obtained. This intensification is most effective when the negative has been dried. It is first bleached in the mercury solution, when it is taken out and washed for half-an-hour. It is then placed in the cyanide of silver solution till the bleaching at the back of the film gives place to a black.

The deposit is a beautiful black by this method, and consists chiefly of a double cyanide of silver and mercury. If left too long in the last bath, intensity diminishes again, owing to the cyanide of mercury being slightly soluble in the bath.

If with this intensification the negative is too dense, it can be reduced as much as needs be by immersing it in a dilute solution of sodium hyposulphite (20 grains to the ounce). The whole of the intensity can be taken away by strong hyposulphite, but the action can be arrested at any time by taking it out of the weak solution and washing. The intensified negative, when dry, is a little less intense than when wet. The atmosphere is apt to attack the intensified images, giving them an appearance of "sulphurisation," and when the right density is secured it is well to varnish them with ordinary negative varnish. Careful washing is as necessary in this process as it was in the preceding.

The writer has recently used intensification by bleaching alone, without attempting to blacken the deposit.

The formula used is that given above, where bromide of mercury is shown as the active reagent.

The question comes as to when sufficient density is secured, either in the simply developed or in the intensified negative. Of course it will be said that to take a print from it is the easiest way to ascertain this, and, no doubt, for the inexperienced, this is an excellent way of deciding; but it often happens that a decision has to be made when the appliances for printing are not at hand.

It is a curious fact, which is confirmed by others besides the writer, that the judgment is apt to be misled, when away from one's ordinary dark room, as to the opacity a negative should show. For instance, in taking and developing a series of views on tour, a good deal depends on the quality of negative obtained during the first day as to the standard of density that is looked for. These may often be really too weak, but it will very often happen that they will be thought good for printing, and the remainder will be standardised accordingly. It is a very useful guide to take with one on tour a good printing negative, and from time to time to compare visually the developed negatives with it. It must be recollected that an opacity in the high lights beyond that necessary to give a white in a print, when the bare glass gives the deepest black, is detrimental; a negative carried beyond that opacity will give a harsh print as a rule, and lack that quality which will enable gradation in whites to be shown, when the gradation in the blacks is also rendered—in other words, a harsh print will be produced. In instantaneous photography there is always a tendency to this by the tyro, generally through an endeavour to give too short an exposure.

The most opaque part of the negative—except, perhaps, minute spots illuminated by sunlight, and almost specularly reflected on to the lens—should not have a greater opacity than that which allows $\frac{1}{60}$ to $\frac{1}{70}$ of the light to pass through it. Thus, for instance, if the deepest shadow be represented as bare glass, the opacity (the brightest part) of a white cloud illuminated by full sunlight should not show more than that density if sky and landscape are to be rendered in the print.

The method of making a scale of shade has been shown in a previous chapter, and it will suffice to have such an one, and print it, say, in platinum, but printing so that the bare glass shall attain the deepest black possible, and then to note which is the first opaque part, where no action is apparent when compared with the whiteness of the unexposed platinum paper. This can easily be done by placing in the printing frame, between the negative and the platinum paper, a strip of black paper along it, masking a portion of the various gradations obtained. The opacity which indicates this equality in whiteness is noted, and the greatest opacities of the negative can be compared with it in a very ready manner. Make two or three fine ink dots on a piece of white paper, and the eye will judge of the distinctness of them when seen through the particular part of the scale of shade which was marked. The same dots are then viewed through the most opaque parts of the negative, and a judgment is rapidly formed of the opacity of its deposit. One can estimate relative opacities to within 5 per cent. by this plan with a little practice.

There are methods which can accurately measure these differences in opacity, one of which is given in

"Instruction in Photography," and as it is measured under the same conditions in which a print is taken, it is very trustworthy; but for purposes of judging density approximately, the above plan is sufficiently accurate. The writer would then recommend that a graduated scale be prepared, as given at page 53, and a strip of such containing the various opacities taken as a guide. It may be remarked that a scale of opacity prepared on a celluloid film is convenient, as it can be carried without any fear of damage or breakage. The writer carries one such in his pocket-book.

Of course, what has been said regarding the opacity needful must be taken only as a general rule. Particular cases require particular treatment. Thus if the beauty of a view consists in getting detail and force in what would be the half-tones ordinarily, the sky must be sacrificed, and become a blank, as far as gradation is concerned, and the unsatisfactory expanse of white paper representing it be filled in by double printing from a cloud negative. This is recommended by many excellent photographers, but does not appeal to the present writer as desirable. This, however, is merely a matter of opinion for which no one person must be held responsible. The ideas of what is artistic are so varied, and the methods of arriving at them so different, that it would be a bold man to lay down any fixed rule concerning any one plan. From a scientific point of view, however, the method of double printing seems a departure from attaining that truth at which photographers should aim.

CHAPTER XIV.

A FEW words must be said on choosing a view with a hand-camera. There is no doubt that a photograph should embrace that part of the general view which appeals most to the eye; but it must be recollected that in the appeal to the eye, its training should be such that the view is divested of colour in thought. Probably a very fair estimate of a view is obtained by looking at it through a greenish blue glass, which cuts off the red and the yellow rays, and leaves it approximately a monochrome. Colour is very often deceptive, particularly in spring and autumn. The eye will see colours contrasted with one another, and it is these contrasts alone which have a real pictorial value, the composition playing almost a secondary part. Divested of colour, a view such as this, when photographed, must be necessarily disappointing; but a glance through a medium such as that recommended will at once tell us what to expect. Constant practice will, however, enable one to do without this aid, and when such experience has been arrived at it is a relief. The view-finder attached to a camera is an excellent device, and certainly every beginner should have one attached to his hand-camera;

but here again it is unnecessary to the experienced
operator.   His training enables him to judge of the
angle of view which his camera will take horizontally
and vertically, and if a couple of lines be ruled on the
top of it, showing the angle included, he will rarely make
a mistake.   He can then point his camera in the
direction required, and attend to that indispensable
adjunct to it—viz., the spirit level, which will tell him
not only whether his camera is level, but will also
indicate to him when it is steady enough to make an
exposure.   But if a view-finder has to be used—and in
nine cases out of ten it should—the great point is to
have a suitable one which can be readily inspected even
in brilliant sunshine.   There are various kinds in the
market, but none seem better, or so good, as that made
on the principle of the magnifying glass, in which an
image is formed by one small lens, and vertically looked
at through a fixed magnifying lens, the image being
reflected by a mirror upwards.   In this instrument
there is no movement of the image when the eye is
moved, as is the case when the finder is a concave
mirror.   The view can be seen in the brightest sunlight,
which is not the case when the images are viewed on a
ground glass, even when shaded by a hood.
    The view having been seen in the view-finder,
whatever is used, the eye should at once take in the
position that the bubble of the level occupies ; and here
let it be said that the circular spirit level is better than
two straight levels placed at right angles to one another,
as with it only one bubble has to be watched, while in
the latter case the position of two has to be taken in by
the eye.   It is probable, when the bubble is central, that

there will be too much foreground, in which case the rising front of the camera must be used to cut off a portion, and a little practice will tell the operator how much of that seen in the finder will disappear, and how much of the sky be added. The appearance of the image will also be a good guide as to the stop to be used, and of the speed to which the shutter should be set. If a small neutral-tinted graduated image be interposed between the eye and the image, and the brilliancy be diminished till it has a brilliancy to which one is accustomed, these may be arrived at with great certainty; but, as before said, it is better to alter the stop rather than the speed of the shutter. Of course it is not necessary with every view to take these measures, otherwise a passing effect would often be lost.

A golden rule to carry out always is, as far as possible, keep the camera level, and use the rising front if necessary. Dismiss all colour from the mind, and have some one point of interest in the view. The writer has often seen excellently taken views, each of which would have cut up into two and sometimes three views, each of which would have been complete in itself. Have some dark points as well as light points in the composition, for one will help the other. If there are none of the former, the print will be flat and washy. In instantaneous work, as in any other photography, if 100 plates are exposed, don't label all as excellent. Technically, perhaps, nine out of ten may be good, but probably of these nine, five or six should be washed off.

The small sized plates cost but little, and there is an inclination to " let off " a-many. This is very good for the plate makers, but fatal for the education of the photographer. A view should be every bit as carefully selected as if a camera or a stand were being used, and time exposure given; and these snap-shots, exposed almost for pure " cussedness," are to be reprobated. The Chancellor of the Exchequer would reap a handsome amount if he taxed every snap-shot made to no purpose. The thing to do is to think over the view, and, when thought over, to make the best possible picture out of it. These are views which will not meet with approval by many, but they are recorded as a deliberate expression of opinion.

CHAPTER XV.

THERE is a kind of instantaneous photography which, however, is not dependent on a shutter, and that is where the illumination itself is instantaneous, or rather, perhaps, it should be said, of short duration. That with which photographers are most familiar is the "magnesium flash-light," where, as the name denotes, the light is produced by burning magnesium in powder. We may have a colourless flame, say, of a spirit lamp, and by some means or another cause the powder to cross it; the heat is sufficient to effect the ignition of the magnesium, and the production of a momentary intensely bright light. Experiments have been made by the writer to ascertain the photographic value of the light caused by the burning of a grain of magnesium compared with that of the electric light. In a communication to the Camera Club, in 1891, he gave the details of these experiments, and we need only give an extract as to the results obtained. It was found that 1 grain of magnesium burnt was equal to 2·16 candles of the whiteness of the electric arc light, burning for one minute, as an illuminant. Sunlight may be taken roughly as twice that of the electric light for each visual candle, and is thus approximately that 1 grain of magnesium is equal to the photographic value of about one visual candle of sunlight acting for one minute. As there are about 5,000 visual candles in sunlight, if such a number could be placed one foot from a screen (at which distance the magnesium was also burned), it follows that 5,000 grains of magnesium, burned at one foot distance from an object, would equal the photographic illumination of sunlight acting for one minute— that is, if a piece of platinum paper were exposed for one minute to the sun, the same blackness on development would be produced by igniting 5,000 grains of magnesium at one foot from it. To produce a good instantaneous picture in sunlight we may take, perhaps, the $\frac{1}{30}$ of a second, with a stop of $f/32$, as necessary, and the equivalent of that would be $\frac{1}{3000}$ of 5,000 grains, or $\frac{5}{3}$ of a grain, or 1·67 grains of magnesium burnt at one foot off. If we place the object ten feet off, we should require 100 times as much, or about 170 grains. For flash-light work a lens working with $f/8$ may be used with advantage, in which case we should only require the $\frac{1}{16}$ of that quantity, or, say, 10 grains. It will be noticed that no mention is made of the time of exposure with the magnesium. It matters very little whether the exposure last a long or a short time; the only requisite is that the necessary amount of magnesium should be burnt. As a matter of fact, the duration of a flash varies very much, but, as a rule, it lasts, when 10 grains are burnt in a proper lamp, about the one-eighth of a second. The diagram (Fig. 28, page 92) shows the measure of a flash. A plate was rotated about once in the one-fourth of a second in front of a small hole cut

in a card.   A sector with only four apertures was
caused to rotate in front of the hole, and the flash impressed the plate as shown.   The effective part of the
flash occupied only eleven intervals of the passage of the
apertures of the sector in front of the hole, and as the
speed of rotation was 20 times a second, 80 apertures
passed per second; the total effective exposure was,

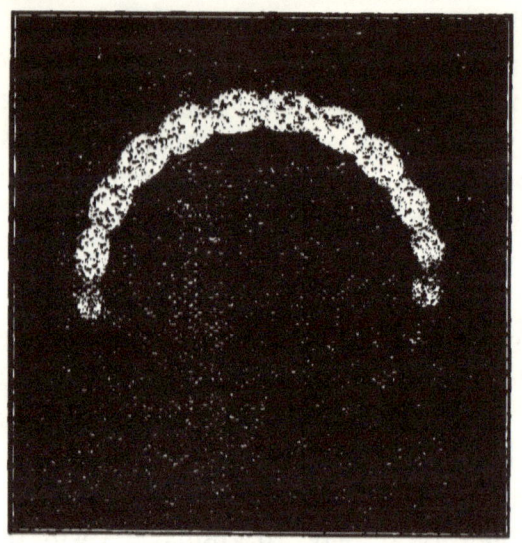

Fig. 28.

therefore, $\frac{11}{80}$ of a second, say $\frac{1}{8}$ of a second.   This
quantity of magnesium is sufficient to photograph an
object 10 feet off when the light is judiciously reflected,
and the exposure in this case would be about one-eighth
of a second.   By connecting two or more lamps
together by rubber tubing, and placed at different
distances so as to break up the shadows, and sending
the magnesium through each flame at the same instant—

which is effected by the india-rubber tubes being connected—the lighting is better, and results can be obtained
which are not to be despised as artistic productions.

We may, however, employ the spark from a battery
of Leyden jars for a certain class of photographs; for
instance, when we wish to photograph waves of sound
or falling drops of water. The arrangement for this is
very simple :—

FIG. 29.

The knobs A A of the spark apparatus are connected
with Leyden jars, which can be charged by a Wimshurst
or other electric machine. The lens L_1 is placed to
condense the spark and cast its image on the centre of
the camera lens L_2. This causes a disc of light to
fall on P, the plate, where the spark passes. The
object O, which is to be photographed, is focussed
on to P. In case of a moving object, the appearance it
has when the spark passes is photographed within the
illuminated disc. The amount included depends on
the diameter of L_1 and the closeness of O to L_1. Or a
stream of falling water may be photographed, and the
separation into drops will be well shown. There are,
in fact, an endless variety of scientific experiments
which may be carried out by this means.

For some purposes the simple shadow method may
be employed in the way that Lord Rayleigh and Prof.
Boys have carried out so successfully. No lens is

employed, but the object whose shadow is to be depicted
is caused to fall or move near the plate, an exposure is
made by the spark, and it being practically a point, the
shadow images are fairly sharp and defined. The
writer prefers the camera method to this last, since it
prevents the difficulty of exposing in a dark room.
The definition, too, is better. The drawback to the
camera method is that it is limited to the movement
which takes place within the area of the condensing
lens L_1. The accompanying diagram gives the position
of bubbles of air blown in a cell of water.

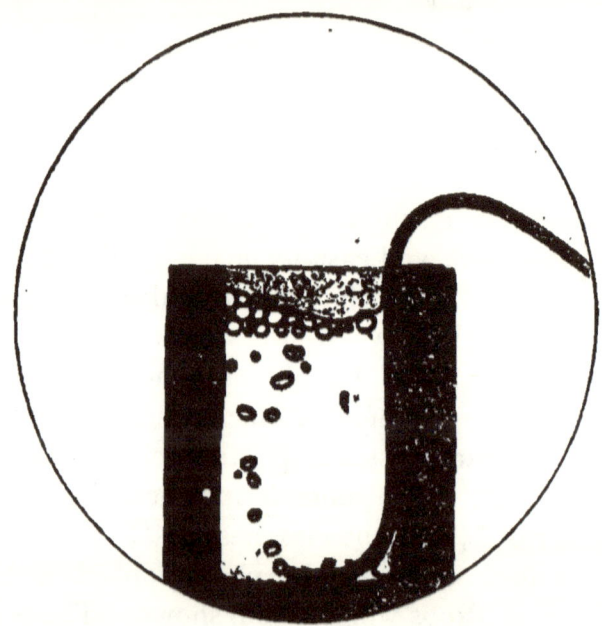

FIG. 30.

For opaque objects the spark light may be condensed
in a circle by means of L_1 on the object, and the camera
be placed alongside the discharging knobs A A. It is
needless to say that the illumination is very inferior to

that obtained by the method shown in the figure, and may not always be successful. The time of exposure is certainly less than the $\frac{1}{100000}$ of a second in this case. A disc with a clean cut series of holes four inches from the centre was rotated 80 times a second, and the spark exposure given to it, a sensitive photographic plate being placed behind it. The velocity of each hole was thus about 2,000 inches per second. A movement during the time of exposure equal to the $\frac{1}{100}$th of an inch would easily have been recognised, but each hole was shown perfectly sharp : the time during which the spark lasted was therefore less than $\frac{1}{200000}$ of a second, so that the limit above stated is certainly under the mark.

These remarks as to flash-light and spark photography have only been given as suggestive, and must not be considered by any means as a complete description of them.

WEIGHTS AND MEASURES.

1 Sovereign weighs...	...	123·274 grains
1 Shilling „	...	87·273 „
48 Pence „	...	1 lb. avoirdupois
Half-penny and Three-penny piece weigh	...	$\frac{1}{4}$ ounce
Florin and Sixpence	...	$\frac{1}{2}$ „
Three Pennies	...	1 „
4 Half-crowns and 1 Shilling	...	2 ounces
4 Florins, 4 Half-crowns, 2 Pennies ...	...	4 „
1 Half-penny = 1 inch in diameter.		

AVOIRDUPOIS WEIGHT.

$27\frac{11}{32}$ Grains	1 drachm (=	$27\frac{11}{32}$ grains)
16 Drachms	1 ounce (=	$437\frac{1}{2}$ „)
16 Ounces	1 pound (=	7000 „)

TROY WEIGHT.

24 Grains	1 pennyweight (=	24 grains)
20 Pennyweights	1 ounce (=	480 „)
12 Ounces	1 pound (=	5760 „)

OLD APOTHECARIES' WEIGHT (superseded in 1864).

20 Grains	1 scruple (=	20 grains)
3 Scruples	1 drachm (=	60 „)
8 Drachms	1 ounce (=	480 „)
12 Ounces	1 pound (=	5760 „)

The New Apothecaries' Weight is the same as Avoirdupois.

LIQUID MEASURE.

60 Minims	1 drachm	
8 Drachms	1 ounce =	1·73 cub. ins. nearly
20 Ounces	1 pint =	34·66 „ „
8 Pints	1 gallon =	277·25 „ „

The Imp. Gallon is exactly 10 lbs. Avoir. of pure water; the pint, $1\frac{1}{4}$ lb.

FLUID MEASURE.

1 Minim =	1 drop	2 Drs. =	1 dessert spoonful
1 Drachm =	1 teaspoonful	4 „ =	1 table „

FRENCH MEASURES.

1 Gramme ...	15·432 grains	
Kilogramme ...	1000 grammes	(=2·2 lbs. Avoir. nearly)
1 Litre...	35·216 ounces (fluid)	
1 Cubic Centimetre (c.c.) ...	17 minims nearly	
{ 50 Cubic Centimetres	1 ounce 6 drachms 5 minims	
1 Metre	39·37 inches	

INDEX.

H

CARTER & Co., Printers, 5, Furnival Street, Holborn, London, E.C.